THE
HAVEN

THE
HAVEN

CAROL LYNCH WILLIAMS

 ST. MARTIN'S GRIFFIN ≋ NEW YORK

THE HAVEN. Copyright © 2014 by Carol Lynch Williams.
All rights reserved. Printed in the United States of America. For information, address St. Martin's Press, 175 Fifth Avenue, New York, N.Y. 10010.

www.stmartins.com

Designed by Anna Gorovoy

The Library of Congress Cataloging-in-Publication Data is available upon request.

ISBN 978-0-312-69871-3 (hardcover)
ISBN 978-1-250-02253-0 (e-book)

St. Martin's Griffin books may be purchased for educational, business, or promotional use. For information on bulk purchases, please contact Macmillan Corporate and Premium Sales Department at 1-800-221-7945, extension 5442, or write specialmarkets@macmillan.com.

First Edition: March 2014

10 9 8 7 6 5 4 3 2 1

To my sixth girl,
Cassidy Silversmith

THE
HAVEN

HAVEN
HOSPITAL & HALLS
Where You Matter
Established 2020

Welcome to:

Blake Green—Faculty
Bonnie Iverson—Faculty
Maria Lopez—Nutritionist

HAVEN
HOSPITAL & HALLS
Where You Matter
Established 2020

Note to all Staff

Please make sure you are present for removals.

1

They came during lunch. They always do. You know, to get one of us.

We bent over our plates of grilled salmon, fresh green beans, and blueberries with cantaloupe. Close enough to whisper. Close enough to touch, if we dared. I could smell the olive oil used to cook the fish. My mouth watered. I couldn't wait to start eating. In my mind I chowed down this fuel, making my body stronger (I hoped). A better performer (I hoped). Well.

Abigail, someone I've known as long as we can both remember, leaned toward me. "It's like you're eating with your nose," she said. "Like some kind of Smell-O-Vision or scratch and sniff."

"Either works," I said. Ms. Iverson, who monitors our table, makes sure we eat, and helps Miss Maria set out our Tonics, nodded over her plate like she wanted to eat, too.

A younger Terminal, not yet eight years old, stood.

"About time," I said in a loud whisper.

"Glorify this food to give us strength," the male said.

"Glorify this food to give us strength." We spoke in unison.

"Glorify this food to cure our ills."

"Glorify this food to cure our ills."

"Glorify this food to make us Whole."

"Glorify this food to make us Whole."

"Glorify this food to make us perfect for the good of our Benefactors."

"Glorify our Benefactors," we said, touching our foreheads.

The Terminal sat and the sounds of talking and silverware clinking on china filled the dining room.

I took a bite of the melon we grow here at Haven Hospital & Halls. It tasted sweet like summer sometimes is, though outside a snowstorm headed our way.

It was right after that tiny bite that the side doors to the cafeteria (the ones used only *then*) opened. These doors, almost as tall as the ceiling, and without windows, squeaked out a warning, but it was as if someone had dropped one of the lead crystal vases filled with flowers. The whole lunchroom went dead quiet. Just like that, hushed. I wasn't sure I could take a complete breath.

"No no no." My hands went cold, and without saying another word, I clasped them together to keep them from shaking.

In the whole of the cafeteria no one seemed to move. Nothing could be heard, though I wondered if my heart was as loud to others as it sounded to me. Were their hearts beating like mine? Two hundred plus of us in here, add in the Staff and Teachers, and not one noise, just beating hearts, maybe *pounding* hearts. The whole group looking at those gigantic doors opening. The light from an eastern window blinded me and then I could see.

Ms. Iverson stood, scraping her chair on the tiled floor, then sat down like she had made a mistake. Mr. MacGee reached out to her.

They aren't supposed to touch. It's bad for us to see that. But they did, a brief finger-to-hand contact.

"Good afternoon, Terminals," Dr. King said as he walked in through the double doors. He strode across the floor, and did that weird thing with his mouth, stretching it up at the corners. His voice was thin, lost in this room full of bodies and plush chairs, a room with tapestries on the walls, flowers everywhere. He waved like he was on parade or something, the sides of his lab coat fluttering because he took such big steps. That sunlight shone on his light-colored hair when he passed beneath it.

Right behind him came Principal Harrison, our pal, everyone's pal. His ponytail bounced as he walked and his suit was neat, crisp. They hurried to the stage, climbing the stairs two at a time, like maybe they wanted to get this over with.

Did *their* hearts pound?

Just last month I practiced on that stage for the part of Nurse in *Romeo and Juliet,* a play about true sacrifice and giving. It seemed so long ago.

Mr. Tremmel, another teacher, ran for the handheld microphone from the china cabinet drawer.

We watched. Blood coursed through my veins like it wanted to get free. No, *I* wanted to get free. Run. Runrunrun. My feet shuffled.

Time slowed and sped up at the same moment as Dr. King and Principal Harrison stepped center stage, moving faster than any Terminal could. My hands clenched so that my fingernails dug into my palms. What would they say? Who would they call?

Abigail reached for me. Brushed her arm against mine. My head spun with a sudden dizziness and my stomach squeezed in on itself.

I thought, *If I can count to a hundred before they start speaking. Yes, count. Onetwothreefourfivesixseven . . .*

7

Dr. King and Principal Harrison are Whole—like our Teachers—
and they scare me. Hearing the doctor's name can make my tongue
go dry as hot sand.

... *twentyonetwentytwotwentythreetwentyfour* ...

Run! Stay! Count!

My throat went so tight, I thought that bit of lunch might come
back up. I could taste cantaloupe again. No longer sweet—now it
had the flavor of strong herbs or bad medicine.

... *Say each number, don't skip, don't skip*

... *thirtyeightthirtyninefortyfortyonefortytwoforty* ...

"Not us," Abigail said. Her voice almost didn't make it the few
inches to me. "Please not anyone I know." She closed her eyes, then
opened them again.

Someone, a little male on the opposite side of the room where all
the males sit, let out a cry, and all at once three of the younger Terminals near him wailed out this inhuman sound, mouths and eyes wide
open. Dr. King, standing at the front of the room now, tried to quiet
them with hushed tones into the microphone. He motioned for their
table monitor to help.

... *sixtysixtyonesixtytwo* ...

"We have reports back now for ... ," Dr. King said. He held up a
manila envelope stuffed with paper and flapped it in the air.

"Stop that fussing," Principal Harrison said. He pointed in the
direction of the wailing males.

... *seventyfiveseventysixseventyseven* ...

Mr. Tremmel leaned over their chairs. I could see him speaking.
Two of the males quieted. The third did, too. But his mouth and eyes
stayed open—wide. He gripped the table. His hair was blond as the
edge of the winter sun.

The whole room felt trapped inside me, along with numbers. My
skin felt raw, worried.

8

I hadn't done it. Hadn't counted fast enough. I would leave again or maybe Abigail. Miss Maria leaned in from the kitchen to watch.

". . . reports are back for Isaac."

The mic hummed, and a few Terminals murmured.

Isaac.

It wasn't me. I wouldn't go. A headache throbbed behind my temples, then left like it exited my ears.

Rituals, I had read in *The Terminal Encyclopedia* (and the words were now stuck in my head), *were believed and practiced by some cultures, though this practice ended the American Terminal culture as we know it.*

I thought, *My counting ritual worked.*

Dr. King stretched his mouth at us again, making his lips into that frightening half moon, then blew into the microphone and continued. "Isaac, after your meal, please go straight to your room. Someone will be waiting for you there. You'll need your prepared bag, as you know." He tapped the envelope. "I hope you all have your bags packed and at the ready. Do you?"

We nodded. The whole group of us.

Isaac, tall and red-haired, sat three chairs down from Gideon, who was Romeo in the play. Gideon. My stomach dropped into my lap. What now? First my heart racing, now my stomach lurching when I looked at this male. Definite signs of illness.

Isaac gave Dr. King a nod. Isaac's lips were pinched—his freckles bright on his now-pale face. A Teacher near him laid a hand on Isaac's shoulder and he curled forward then shrugged the Teacher away. Isaac stood, shaking his head like he wanted to clear it, and walked for the doors that led from the dining room. The regular doors that would take him to his bedroom. He took one last look at us all.

Isaac was leaving.

I swallowed.

I am not.

He raised his hand in an almost-salute and went into the hall.

He hadn't even finished eating. The most important part of any Terminal's day—consuming our nutrients—and he left a full plate behind.

Principal Harrison took the microphone from the doctor and said, "No gloomy faces here. We must keep the rest of you healthy, now, mustn't we? Eat up. Only the best food, only the best care for you here at Haven Hospital and Halls. Clean your plates. We always recycle, reuse, and never let anything go to waste."

No one made a sound.

Don't move, don't even breathe, and they may not see you, I thought.

The doctor and our principal left the room, going the way they had come, through the big doors that closed, this time, without a sound. Everyone took on life as minutes crept by. Terminals spoke to each other, soft at first, then the noise level grew.

I didn't have the strength to pick up my fork. Abigail tapped the back of my hand. My head spun.

"Eat, Shiloh. Abigail," Ms. Iverson said, from the far end of the table. "Lunch will be over soon. We don't need you growing weak, too."

"Yes, Shiloh," said Abigail. Her forehead wrinkled. She got close enough for our cheeks to touch, though not quite. I slid away. "What would I do if you weren't with me?"

I blinked to make the dizziness go away.

"Don't ask that," I said.

Abigail nodded. "I shouldn't think of anything outside of Haven Hospital and Halls, but sometimes I do. Like, what I would do if you were gone?" Her voice dropped to a whisper. "I wish we didn't live here."

I gulped nothing but air.

"That's preposterous. We're Terminals," I said, drawing out the word. "This is where we live."

Abigail picked up her fork and pulled a bit of the salmon apart. "If," she said. "What about *if* we didn't?"

I shrugged. "I don't know. I've never thought of being away from here."

What do we expect at Haven Hospital & Halls? We are Terminal. I know this. We *all* know this. We leave. We take our prepared bags sometimes and go. But not like Abigail suggested. Like Isaac now. That kind of leaving is part of us.

"Imagine being free," Abigail said. She whispered the words but they felt so loud, everyone in the Dining Hall must have heard them.

"Don't say that," I said. Her words made me uncomfortable. "It could have been you and saying this might make it you." The thought of Abigail being called away was almost as bad as the thought of *me* being the next one taken out for Treatment.

You never know.

There is no pattern that I can distinguish. I remember everyone who's left. And when, too. That information sticks in my brain. Things I need to remember (and things I don't) stay around longer for me than for other Terminals, even with the Tonic.

"We never know who or when or why," I said.

Ruth, sitting on the other side of me, said, "We do know." Her huge brown eyes seemed even bigger than normal. "The Disease may strike at any moment, any time. We have to be prepared. We stay here and prepare for the worst."

Abigail didn't answer.

"We're lucky to live here." Ruth pointed with her knife. "Haven Hospital and Halls is the finest Treatment center available."

Around us the noise in the dining room became a steady hum. Had the Terminals already forgotten about Isaac? Memories the medication should keep away were still close enough for me to touch.

11

Long ago, I quit telling Dr. King how much I remembered, because the increase in Tonics made me so sick, I couldn't eat.

It's best to keep some things to myself.

No one needs to know what's in my head.

That irreverent thought made me want to tell on myself, but I pushed it away.

"Eat. Keep strong," Ruth said. She ate like her words would keep her from leaving again.

Now Abigail's lips were thin and white, like the blood had seeped from them. I brushed my fingertip against her arm, a quick touch, though it meant a burst of nausea. Her skin was as cold as if nothing ran through her veins.

"Ruth's right, Abigail," I said, and Ruth nodded. "You've heard the doctors. The better health we have, the better chance we have."

Abigail turned to her food.

And though I wasn't sure it *would* help, I finished lunch.

2

"All right, everyone," Ms. Iverson said once we settled into our chairs for English. Some Terminals stared at their desktops. It's like this when someone goes, like our batteries are drained. Terminals might not remember who was gone, but when those Dining Hall doors open, an awful feeling stays with us, if only for a few hours.

Now Ms. Iverson closed our classroom door, stood facing the opaque glass, then turned and gazed out at all of us. She spoke to the tops of bent heads.

"Let's chat." Her voice was low, desktop level.

She does this every time someone we know leaves. Isaac is in this class with us. (Or was? Should I say was?) I tried to gather courage from somewhere that seemed empty inside, then looked back at Ms. Iverson again.

"You know we can't spend a lot of time on this subject, but we'll talk for a few minutes."

I pressed my knuckles to my lips, eyes stinging. Maybe if I didn't blink, I might be safe the next time those doors opened.

No blinking.

Counting.

Eating even when I wasn't hungry.

All to save myself.

Maybe.

No.

All this at Haven Hospital & Halls is good. It might all be a saving grace, though there is no grace for Terminals living at this Treatment center that doubles as a school.

I pretended to listen to Ms. Iverson. I didn't *want* to hear what she said. I had this speech memorized.

Voices took turns around me, but I kept my head down. Focused on the lined paper stacked on the corner of my desk.

More than twenty Terminals had been in and out of surgery since my own operation. Twenty Terminals in about a year.

The computations were easy. Nearly two per month.

I rubbed a finger over my palm.

None had seemed ill.

When someone is contagious, they're quarantined, put into Isolation. But even then we won't be called away.

The Disease, they told us, was silent, never showed its head, seemed instead to be hidden in the lab reports that Dr. King brought with him.

13

And I knew for a fact, *I* had been healthy. I hadn't felt ill. There were no hints. No indication of trouble.

Then, without warning, *my* name was called. My fingertips went numb, remembering.

I closed my eyes again. The Terminals around me spoke in soft voices.

I relived leaving more often than not. The way my name was called. How I hadn't accepted the summons at first and Dr. King had to call my name again. How I had stood at that lunch. How my knees shook. Abigail said, "Be strong." And I walked across the Dining Hall at the end of the meal with everyone watching and Mr. MacGee nodding to me, like a good-bye. When I had looked at the Terminals and it was like we were all the same person because it would happen to them and it was happening to me and it had happened to others before.

For decades.

That's what Dr. King said.

Now, at the front of the classroom as Ms. Iverson spoke in subdued tones, I peered at the two bare poplars outside the window, out at the spring snow. Isaac walked tall when he left the dining room today. I'm not so sure I had.

"No more!" A voice jarred me.

Gideon stood beside his chair. His face was blotchy. He looked so . . . what? Sick?

"Gideon," Ms. Iverson said. She went across the room to stand near him but didn't get too close.

"There has to be a promise," Gideon said. He spoke through clenched teeth. His sandy-colored hair fell over his forehead, curled a little at his collar. He was at least a head taller than Ms. Iverson and even from where I sat I could see how blue his eyes were. My insides tumbled seeing him.

"Are you okay?" Ms. Iverson's hands were extended, like she might touch him, though I knew she wouldn't unless extreme measures were called for and Security came.

Gideon swung toward her. I'd never seen a Terminal move like that. He was so fast. "Am I okay? No!" His voice grew. I covered my ears.

Three Terminals at the front of the classroom—Camille, Ruth, and John—slid back in their chairs like they were afraid. Matthew dropped his book. It landed on the floor with a pop and half the classroom jumped, including me.

"You have reason to be upset, Gideon," Ms. Iverson said. Her hands still out. Her voice soothing.

"This is wrong," he said, and I uncovered my ears. His voice was quiet now—like what he would say was meant for only a few of us to hear, and not the whole class. "It doesn't have to be this way."

No one replied.

"What're you saying, Gideon?" Abraham asked. "This is the way and the life."

"We're Terminals," Sarah said. She twisted her short hair around her finger, and whispered, "We're Terminals." Twist, twist, twist.

"I know that, Sarah," Gideon said. He took a step and she flinched. "We *all* know that. But what we don't know is why. Why does it have to be that way? Why us?"

Ms. Iverson checked the door, then the window.

"Why can't there be a promise?" Gideon walked to the front of the classroom, walked back to his chair. He ran his hands through his hair. He moved so fast—his gestures, his steps, were like the silly movies we sometimes see on Terminal Television. "Why can't there be cures? Why can't *we* . . . the Terminals"—his words hovered in the air—"find answers?"

Ms. Iverson's face turned red. "We need to get going on Harper

15

Lee's novel. I want to talk about how Atticus's Terminal situation of seeing all people as equal caused trouble for his family."

"No!" Gideon said. Although his voice was soft, it made me draw back. I looked at Abigail, who sits behind me. Her eyes were huge.

"What's happening?" Sarah asked from across the room. "Is he sick? Is he having a breakdown?"

"Maybe we should call for help, Ms. Iverson," Matthew said. "Maybe we need the doctor here. Gideon might be contagious." Matthew tapped on his desktop.

"I don't know, I don't know," someone said.

I covered my eyes. My hands felt cool as water. Fingers spread, I watched as Gideon shoved his desk down the aisle toward the front of the room. It slid on its side. Pencils, books, and a calculator spilled on the wood floor. Outside, a few flakes of snow fell.

"No! I *want* to talk about this."

Daniel rolled forward in his wheelchair. "Gideon," he said. "Stop. Now."

And Gideon stopped. He made a face at Daniel like nothing I had never seen, righted the chair where it had landed, and sat a foot and a half from Ms. Iverson's desk. I would have been self-conscious with such close proximity to a Teacher. Sick, even.

"He wants a cure," Daniel said to Ms. Iverson. He took off his glasses, then put them back on. "He wants a cure. I do. We all do, right?" He looked around the classroom.

No one moved.

"Yes." Abigail's voice was weak.

I squeezed my hands together. Something heavy sat in my chest.

Twice in one day. Too much excitement. Too much moving and yelling and calling Terminals out.

Calm down, Shiloh, I thought. *Or you'll follow Isaac to the hospital.*

16

"We'll wait a moment on *To Kill a Mockingbird*," Ms. Iverson said. She pulled at her shirt a little, like she stretched out invisible wrinkles. Then she patted at her hair.

My whole Terminal world seemed to tilt, like *I* had tipped over and not Gideon's chair.

"Terminal," Ms. Iverson said. "We all know the definition." She put her hands under her chin.

"Who can forget?" Camille asked, shifting in her seat.

Oh, they forgot. If enough time passed, Isaac would not be remembered at all—even if I brought him up to another Terminal.

Maybe my memory is part of my illness, part of my disease. It was a frightening thought.

"I know," Ms. Iverson said. Her eyes grew watery. That's one thing with the Whole. They leak. I saw Ms. Iverson's face leak like right now (and heard her bark like a seal, wearing a horrible expression once while she read. Late one night when I should have been sleeping but had awakened from a nightmare and went to find her for Tonic).

I agreed with Camille. We all know the definition. As soon as we can learn, we're taught the meaning. I watched Gideon, who glowered out the window, like maybe none of us were here. Did he see the snow the same way I had? My insides twisted. Or did he look at those trees that held no promise of spring yet?

Ruth said, "Terminal: of or forming a limit, boundary, or end. Concluding; final. Ending in death; fatal."

I glanced back at Ms. Iverson. "Our lives here will end in death," I said.

Or worse.

"Not if there's a cure." The words one-at-a-time slow. Gideon again.

Could Terminals be cured? It didn't seem possible.

Ms. Iverson's mouth hung open, then, "Good, Ruth," she said. It was as if Gideon hadn't spoken. "And you, too, Shiloh."

"No," Gideon said, the word coming out with a long breath of air. "No, it's not good. 'Ending in death; fatal.' *That* is not good." Gideon did something strange then. Looked around the room, like he wanted to catch our eyes with his. I let my gaze shift to just over his ear.

Then he left the room without permission!

Ms. Iverson's eyebrows went up and she pursed her lips. She said, "Go ahead and start reading, class. I'll be right back." She followed Gideon, closing the door.

The room calmed. Outside, the storm moved closer, the afternoon sky became dark. Dark as Gideon's face had been. Snowflakes fell harder. Changed their minds. Stopped. Fell again.

"What was *that*?" Abraham asked. He sounded uncomfortable.

"Gideon had a mental malfunction," Camille said.

"No," Daniel said. He swung his wheelchair around to face us. He whispered, his eyes wide. "Gideon's right. We never expect anything here *except* to die."

I pulled in a deep breath of air. "That's the truth of our world, Daniel. We've seen it on Terminal Television. We saw it"—I gestured toward the dining room—"just this morning. We all die."

"This is our lives," Ruth said. She shrugged. Her dark, shoulder-length hair swung a bit around her face. "We live away from everyone to keep us alive longer."

"But we don't have to," Daniel said. He still whispered, resting his hands where his legs should have been. "We *could* look for a cure. A way out."

"We could try," Abigail said. Her voice was hesitant, like maybe she tasted these words for the first time.

The need to do what was right stirred in me. We *must* do the right thing. *Must* be obedient. Obedience kept us safe.

"No," I said, "even thinking that kind of thing is wrong."

The classroom door swung open and all talking ceased. Ms. Iverson went to her desk. "No one is to speak of what happened today. Do you understand? Do not speak of this."

A few Terminals nodded.

"Today is our little secret."

Another surprise. Too many for one day. I put my head on my desk, wondering if Ms. Iverson would send Gideon to Isolation and why he and Daniel might think we could do anything, anything at all, to save ourselves.

HAVEN
HOSPITAL & HALLS
Where You Matter
Established 2020

Note to all Staff

Behavior to Look For:
Uncommon socialization
Touching
Fraternizing with the opposite sex
Too much speaking
Open talk of rebellion

Any and all of these (and similar) behaviors MUST be reported to school officials.

3

"One minute to lights out" sounded over the intercom and the music of Brahms was piped into the building. I yawned. A creature of habit, I guess.

I swallowed the plastic cup of Tonic that sat on my bedside table, my prepared bag an arm's length away. Then I climbed into bed. The room grew quiet.

I share this room with three other girls, including Abigail. We're a Dorm unit and as the Disease progresses it takes more and more from some.

Settling under my comforter, I lay still as a shadow, letting the music sweep over me. From my bed I could see out the huge window. Snow fell. Fat flakes that came down like feathers, like they took their time leaving the sky, twisting and turning. Moonlight turned the darkness blue. I shivered and yawned again, then lay on my side.

"I heard Gideon disrupted studies today," Mary said.

"Yes," I said, the word muffled in my pillow. "It happened in my class. He went berserk. Changed into a maniac in front of everyone."

Mary and Abigail sat up.

"And?" Elizabeth said.

"Ms. Iverson got water in her eyes."

"Water?" Mary asked.

I sat, too, so my whispers would cover the distance of the room. "Water poured *from her eyes*." I told them everything, even how Gideon pushed the desk over.

Elizabeth said, "Oh no."

Abigail rested against her pillow in the pale light. "I think he wants out of here," she said.

No one answered.

"Like we all do," I said. The words made me cringe. I didn't quite believe what I spoke. Even with Abigail's questioning, I wasn't so sure I wanted to leave. I know what happens to Terminals in the real world.

"I want to stay where I'm safe," Mary said, echoing my thoughts like she could read my mind.

"But if you didn't *have* to be here," Abigail said. She was going down *that* road again? "If you could be Whole, you would be, wouldn't you?"

There was a long pause. Brahms grew softer. The hall lights dimmed.

"Yes," Mary said.

"We shouldn't talk that way," Elizabeth said.

"No one is supposed to know about the incident," I said.

"All the Terminals do," Elizabeth said. "I heard groups talking about it. But no Teachers. At least not yet."

If anyone found out—any Teacher, I mean—that could mean trouble for Gideon. And even though I wasn't sure if I agreed with what he said, I didn't want him in trouble.

Still, his behavior demanded Isolation.

Isolation is just what it says on the outside of the door: PENITENCE AND REFORM ROOM. A few hours alone, where the white of the walls blinds you, and you're ready to promise anything. At least I had been. I don't ever want to go again. Twice is enough for me.

"I hope no one finds out," Mary said.

"Gideon's tough," Elizabeth said. "I heard Principal Harrison talking to Dr. King."

"What did Principal Harrison say?" This was Abigail.

Elizabeth thought for a long second. "Something about how Gideon is stronger than other Terminals. That he needs to be supervised."

A weight descended on my shoulders just as it always does when anyone speaks of something contrary. "I want to sleep."

We all settled down, but I lay in bed wide-eyed.

The thoughts wouldn't stop.

If I peered out the window, I could see Hall Four. There's a plaza between us, the stilled fountain, a gazebo at the edge of things, and a small courtyard. In the spring it's full of flowers.

If I checked outside now, I'd see the old brick of that arm of the rooms, the wide windows, each with a small balcony. At the west end of the structure, I would see the chimney rising from the building like a finger pointing to the sky.

The males reside in Hall Four. Gideon's room is there.

And Isaac's.

Or it had been.

"Don't think about him," I said.

"Excuse me?"

Abigail moved in bed. "Do you need something, Shiloh?"

"I'm fine," I said.

Lies!

"No more talking tonight," she whispered. "I heard the hall monitors will be out in force to make sure we get our eight hours."

"They always do, every time one of us goes," I said.

"They want to see if we're going to lose it," Abigail said. She paused. "It's all about control, you know."

"Control?"

"I don't understand," Elizabeth said.

The lights went out and the music softened to nothingness. I yawned again. Mary's breathing became heavy and deep. I swear, she can sleep anywhere. One morning, early, I found her snoozing on one of the toilets, her head against the stall wall, pajama bottoms around her ankles.

Abigail lowered her voice. "It's about keeping us calm. So they can do to us what they'll do to Isaac."

Neither Elizabeth nor I spoke.

"Terminals live this way," I said, that same useless reminder. "We live this way."

"I know," Abigail said.

The dimmed light from the hall seeped into the room. I could see the outline shadow of her.

"I know." She lay back.

4

Control? Why would Abigail think *that* word? Didn't it make her ill to say it?

I should go to Abigail.

Tiptoe across the room and crawl into bed with her, lying on top of her comforter, my own blanket covering me so we didn't touch skin to skin. We could wait until Elizabeth was sound asleep. Talk about Isaac. His pale face. About Gideon. His outburst. Daniel's suggestion that Gideon wanted us to have cures for our kind.

Abigail and I could—leave, search the dark halls, sit in the shadows.

My heart kicked up a beat. We've snuck out lots. Got caught only the first time. The consequence was a private meeting with Principal Harrison.

And, Isolation.

Abigail and I had wandered the school, going to the kitchen, where we found all the food locked away.

In the corner bed, Mary snored—she always snores the first ten minutes she's asleep. Elizabeth mumbled something.

If I closed my eyes, I would dream.

I'm tired of the nightmares, I thought. They come more often than not when another Terminal is taken away.

When everyone slept, I threw back the covers and tiptoed to our window, looking out at Hall Four. The windows there were dark and empty, like eyes made only of pupils. I shivered.

That's when I saw the movement. The slightest shift. A dog maybe? But how could an animal get in here? The thing straightened up some and I saw the shape was much bigger than a dog. It was the size of a small bear. Or . . . a Terminal? Something surged up my throat. A Terminal dressed all in black?

A dot of a red light flickered near the shape. Went out. Flickered again.

"What in the world?" My breath made a circle of steam on the window and I wiped it away with the sleeve of my pajamas. Touched the cold glass with my fingertips.

Another flicker of light sparked across the courtyard, near the gazebo at the end of the green.

The figure hurried toward the light and then the moon slid behind a cloud and I couldn't see anything more.

"Who is that?" Today, it seemed, my heart had spent way too much time beating way too hard.

We Terminals don't get afraid. Only Then. Only when the door squeaks open does fear course through us. So why did my heart pound now?

I pressed my hand, cool from the windowpane, onto my side near my scar. Through the fabric of my nightshirt I felt the raised flesh.

"Shiloh," said a whispered voice right next to my ear. "What do you see?"

I let out a yelp and swung, striking Abigail in the shoulder. "Don't ever do that again." I squeezed her elbow. My head swirled and I staggered back, falling against the windowsill. I kept my voice low. "Ever." I moved toward her and gave her a small shake. My stomach roiled and I released her.

"You didn't have to hit me." Abigail peered out into the darkness. "I just wondered what you were looking at. You're supposed to be asleep."

"So are you," I said.

We eyed each other then looked out the window together.

Nothing. Whatever was out there was gone. So were the red flashes.

It could have been an intruder. Sometimes people break onto the school grounds but Security always takes them away.

Two weeks ago. What? What had happened?

The memory of the Incident was almost not there. How the Whole male had run into the Dining Hall, grabbed at a young female Terminal, tried to run off with her. Disturbing, is what Principal Harrison said later, when the male was stopped by our uniformed guards and then dragged away by police from the outside.

"Our apologies," Principal Harrison had said at the microphone. "It is our duty at Haven Hospital and Halls to keep you away from the lunatics."

Was that the same lunatic out in the snow now?

"What did you see?" Abigail cupped her hand around her eyes and leaned against the pane.

The night was black. Only the shapes of the building were visible now. Blocks of darkness. I could see our reflections. I stood a head taller than Abigail, and her hair fell around her shoulders while I'd pulled mine back so it wouldn't be a giant puff ball in the morning. I opened my mouth to tell her what I had seen. Then I hesitated. I *should* tell. It was my duty to answer when asked a question.

"Nothing," I said. "I couldn't sleep." A truth.

She nodded. "The last of winter is so nice, isn't it?" Abigail stood close to me. I could feel the heat of her body. Tension rolled up my throat.

Nice? "Yeah. Maybe," I said.

"I love spring best," she said, padding back to bed. "When everything is new and it seems like even we Terminals have a chance."

A chance.

A promise.

I loved nothing. But I believed what Abigail said.

Spring did feel like a chance.

A promise was what Gideon said we should have. And at that moment, standing halfway between my bed and the window, I believed in that promise, or that chance, too. I wanted to be more than a Terminal. I wanted a life. To live outside the walls. While I wouldn't say so to Abigail, I *did* want a chance to live elsewhere, as one of the Whole.

I checked out the gazebo one last time, straining to see anything, but there wasn't even a glimmer of light. A shiver ran from shoulder to shoulder. I went back to bed and slept.

Do you have your suitcase?

It's there. By my nightstand.

You won't be gone long.

I nod. Walk. It's so far. The corridor is a dark hole. Cold as snow. I walk forever. The blinking light never gets closer.

I'm on the bed. Someone cries out.

The voice echoes. Comes into my mind again and again.

We'll get rid of the Disease. What we can, he says.

Brightness stabs at my eyes. I feel it in the back of my head, it's so sharp. The light turns red. Cuts across the yard.

There's the knife, slicing down my breastbone, opening me up, like chicken in the kitchen when I help cook.

Hands reaching in pull out the blackness that fills me. I feel the dark being torn away. Feel the tendons separating from the bone. Blackness turns red as blood.

They have my heart, dripping what looks like used car oil. Steam rises. I smell something awful.

The red light flickers again. The male in black motions for me to come to the gazebo, but I cannot without my heart.

They sew me up.

But the bleeding will not stop.

5

"Abigail!"

I woke myself, screaming. The cold of my dream followed me into waking. I felt like I had showered in icy water.

I curled in on myself. "Help?" I whispered, testing the air around me. Hearing my own voice calmed me, and the ice in my skin thawed.

"You're okay, Shiloh. It's just the dream again. You're used to it."

But I'm not, even though I dream that same thing all the time.

Our room was dark except for the faint light from the hallway. No one awoke from my crying out. All around me was the sound of steady breathing.

I pulled the comforter to my chin, turned over, and burrowed my face into my pillow.

"You're okay. You're okay," I said. My nerves tried to get into my brain.

I couldn't lose control. A dream wasn't like those Dining Hall doors opening. A dream was my brain releasing stress. That's what Dr. King said once in assembly. I remembered it, word for word.

"We've had a lot of Terminals complaining of nightmares." Dr. King had raised his hands to us like dreams sat on his palms. "This is just your brain relieving the stress of the day. You have no reason to fear your dreams. They mean nothing." He'd worn a dark blue suit that day. And a bow tie. "If they bother you, come to the Nurse's Station for a change in your Tonic. If they continue, we'll see you at the Infirmary."

That was the day I'd decided I'd never go to the Infirmary for help. Not with my worries or my dreams or my memory. I would keep to myself.

"Easy," I said now. "I'll try for nothing. Hope to get my mind off Isaac. Not think of any Terminals."

The best thing I could do now would be:

To not sleep at all.

To have no more dreams.

And to please forget that look on Isaac's face.

A Mozart sonata woke me.

At first I wasn't even sure I could get my eyes open, I was that tired. That deep in sleep. My bedding was warm, and I was warm. The dream had fled and taken with it all the coldness of the night before.

But oh! Isaac. Once again I recalled how his freckles looked so prominent on his all-the-sudden pale skin. I remembered Gideon shoving that chair. Had any other Teachers heard about what happened? Was Gideon learning all about Penitence and Reform at this moment?

You have got to let this go, I thought. *Everyone else forgets. You do it, too. Make yourself forget.*

"All true stories end in the Terminal's death," I said. Ernest Hemingway said those words after he wrote *For Whom the Bell Tolls,* where not one Terminal comes to any good at all.

What I needed to do was think of life. All around me were the sounds of morning. No one else seemed concerned. I threw back the blanket, uncovering my head.

Mary hummed—something she was learning in Band, I bet. Bright snow-light filled the room. Elizabeth sat cross-legged on her bed, a thick book in her lap. She held her long black hair back with one hand.

"Better get up," she said. "You're going to be late. And you know how that can ruin a day. It's almost impossible to catch up if you start out late." She turned a page.

Poor Elizabeth, I thought. *So anal.* She's the smartest Terminal in our hall, though.

"Yeah, Shiloh." Mary went to her dresser. "You know you aren't supposed to be late for breakfast. Plus Abigail wants you to hurry. She's saving you a spot at the table." Mary dug through her drawer, grabbed a pair of blue jeans, then left for the bathroom. Before her surgery she always dressed with Abigail and Elizabeth and me. No one ever says this now, above all not Mary, but I think she's self-conscious because of the amputations.

I stretched, lifting my arms high, feeling a pull in my scar.

Outside, the world seemed as dazzling as the sun reflecting in a mirror. Light poured into the room, puddling on the floor, making the pale carpet seem warm. I stretched again, pointing my toes, and said, "I won't be late. Promise."

"Okay, then," Elizabeth said.

What would it be like to wake up and *not* worry about who might leave Haven Hospital & Halls?

To not have a scar with concerns of more to come?

To not have the dreams?

To only worry about being late?

"Shiloh." Elizabeth stood at the foot of my bed, her book tucked under her arm. I sat up. "You have to go." She regarded me with such intensity that at first I thought maybe she knew my thoughts.

Her standing there like that reminded me of something. What?

The figure.

The bouncing light.

I gripped my blanket. The need to tell boiled up inside. I bit my tongue to keep my mouth shut. "I'm going."

"Great," she said. "I worry that you'll get behind." She was ready, her hair done, her clothes neat and clean, a pink glow to her face. Her eyes looked too green.

I threw back the covers and stepped to the window. The only new thing was this almost-spring snow. Nothing near the gazebo. Not even footprints.

Had I imagined it all?

I went back to the tasks at hand. Made my bed, then pulled out a creamy yellow shirt from my closet.

There was no denying it.

I saw what I saw. Even if I didn't know what it had been, there *was* a light and a figure.

Elizabeth chattered with Mary, who was dressed now and ready for the day.

Had it been a Terminal last night? An animal?

Or someone from the outside?

Cool air swirled near my ankles.

Couldn't be. There was no way. How had they gotten onto the grounds? A huge concrete wall surrounds the institution. There's only one way in, one way out. There's a station where you have to show ID to gain access. Sure, there are visitors, VIPs that walk the grounds, sit in the office with Principal Harrison, or tour the buildings at the back of the property with Dr. King. They check out the kitchen with Miss Maria showing the way. But there are always chaperones. Teachers keep us away from the Visitors, and Security keeps outsiders away from us.

But the Whole do get in here. They have scaled the walls. Once, long before I was sent here to live, someone drove a truck through the gates, demanding money by means of a physical threat. Dr. King told us.

So intruders were a possibility.

But a Terminal outside like that? In the cold? We just aren't built for extreme temperatures.

I couldn't wait any longer. This was a mystery I couldn't solve. I had to get ready for the day.

I know about the concrete wall because of Abigail.

Last summer, she and I went exploring every time we got the chance.

Abigail said, "How far can we follow the wall? It's got to end sometime."

"I've heard it goes on forever," I had said. I shadowed my eyes at the barrier.

That day had been bright. Hot. Flowers bloomed everywhere, both wild and in the greenhouse. They grew in flower beds, all gauzy with color. Dr. King surveyed the whole of Haven Hospital & Halls, hands on his hips. Classes are shorter in warm weather so we can spend time outside and even garden if we want. We're encouraged to enjoy the good air, get the right amount of vitamin D.

"Breathe healthy." That's a rule.

So Abigail and I had walked. We went some distance, past the greenhouses, past the old nursery, past the huge building with glass block windows and the NO ADMITTANCE signs on every entrance.

Way behind us was the murmur of Terminal voices. Four females sat on benches that circled a rose garden. One lifted her face to the sun.

Abigail and I spoke about nothing. It felt like it took forever to reach the wall. I stood there looking at it, head tipped back, hand a visor again. Bees buzzed bushes of lavender, and a grasshopper sat camouflaged on the pampas grasses that were taller than me.

"We're here," I had said.

The memory of that day was bright as could be, squint-your-eyes bright.

Abigail tromped along, head down, steps that sent resting butterflies fluttering to get away.

I patted the wall. The block was warm under my hand, and rough, too. I could smell the scorch of the weeds. I almost forgot why we were outside, then remembered the reason we had set out. "What's on the other side?"

Abigail shrugged.

The sun was comfortable on my shoulders. It shone in Abigail's auburn hair. Did the sun brighten my hair like it did hers? My hair is golden. Did it have the same red colors? "A world without Terminals," I said, and I had felt satisfied.

"Let's look over." Abigail lowered her voice even though we were alone. "You want to boost me?"

"Ummmm," I said. The thought made me jittery. Made me want to leave. Go back closer to the school. Sure, we wondered what was over the wall, but I'd never thought to try and take a peek. The idea made my hands sweat. Made my nerves crawl. "We can't do that. We're not allowed."

"Who ever said?"

I searched my memory. "No one."

Abigail gave me a nod of triumph.

"But it *has* to be wrong."

She hesitated only a second like she carried on an argument with herself. "That's why we should look."

Between us and that last group of Terminals was a large expanse of field. We'd waded through wildflowers and spots of colors. No one seemed to notice us.

Abigail ran her hand over the creamy-colored stucco.

She had a point. There are plenty of rules here—to keep us as healthy as a Terminal can be. The list went on and on. But no one had said, *Do not climb the wall.*

Ever.

"You help me," Abigail said. The smell of summer filled the air. Flowers bobbed their rainbow heads.

I let out a nervous sound. "Are you sure?"

"You know it. There's no one around, we're as far away from the main buildings as we can get. This will be interesting. In fact—" Abigail got in my face. My stomach swirled. "—this is learning about our—" She paused. "—our environment."

Hmmm.

"If you put it that way."

That day, I pushed Abigail as high as I could without touching her skin. But she hadn't been quite strong enough to reach to the top of the wall. The Disease had taken part of her arm earlier and she was still recovering.

Abigail grabbed for the top, but couldn't hold on one-handed.

"Let me down, Shiloh," she said. She dropped to the ground. Her cheeks were pink. "Let me get you up there."

"Are you sure? I'm heavier than you. Can you do it?" By now I could almost imagine what was on the other side. Probably a mansion. Or a castle. Or maybe a table piled high with fine foods. My mouth watered. I was thirsty.

"You have to see for both of us," Abigail said, bending at the waist. "Climb up on my back." She leaned against the wall, holding herself steady. I slipped off my shoes, my socks still on, and stepped onto her back, unsteady and nervous. My feet slid on her shirt and I could feel her ribs. I hugged the surface for balance.

"Too short," I said, the familiar feeling of disobedience spreading in my chest.

Abigail moved under me, trying to keep her balance. "Get up on my shoulders," she said, already winded.

I looked at her. "I could hurt you."

"We can't let all my therapy be for nothing." She sounded just like Ms. Seabold, the physical therapist.

"Terminals," I said, mimicking Ms. Seabold, "I don't spend my valuable time helping you increase your health for nothing. Exercise! Eat right! Use sunscreen!"

"See?" Abigail said. "She *wants* us to look over."

I climbed to Abigail's shoulders. The top of the wall was still too high. But if I reached up, and if she pushed and I scrambled . . .

Abigail wiggled a bit.

"Hold still," I said, grunting.

I pulled myself up, scratching my hands and then my belly. With a foot on Abigail's shoulder, I pushed toward the ledge. With my other foot, I tried to get myself a little higher.

I could see. There was a field of wildflowers, like the ones that grew here. A small stream caught the sunlight and threw it back, sparkling, into the air.

Abigail, sounding like she had no oxygen left, said, "Hurry. What do you see?"

"Flowers. Trees. There's a fence with wires at the top. And something past that. Oh. A lot of people. Carrying signs, it looks like. Hard to see."

"What do the signs say?"

"How would I know?" I said. "They're too far away. And smaller than your thumb." I struggled to hang on, to see anything past the fence. My toes scratched at the wall, trying to find a place to hold my weight.

"Which thumb?" Abigail asked. "The one I have or the one I don't have?"

"Don't be such a Terminal. There's a lot of the Whole. And cars with flashing lights on top." I thought for a second. "Police

38

cars. I remember from Terminal Television when we had that intrusion."

"You two!"

Abigail jolted, turning under my foot. I felt her struggle to remain beneath me but she fell away. I clawed at the thick top part of the wall. In slow motion, I slid down the stuccoed block.

"What is going on here?" It was Ms. Iverson, I could tell by her voice. She was brand-new to the Haven Hospital & Halls.

"Move, Abigail," I said, my cheek against the wall, my fingers losing their grip. I heard her roll away and I slid the rest of the way to the ground.

"Ow," I said when I landed.

"We were trying to see what's on the other side," Abigail said from flat on her back. Her ponytail lay like a rope out across the grass.

The tips of my fingers were raw and I had even skinned my chin and one side of my face. My toes felt bruised.

"The world is out there," Ms. Iverson had said. She patted the wall, making the sound you get when you thump an unripe watermelon. "And this is to keep you two safe. Germs from over there might infect you."

"Right," Abigail said. She stood, brushed off her shirt and pants, looked at me under half-closed eyelids.

My fingertips stung. I put my shoes back on. Ms. Iverson sent me to the Infirmary, where Nurse fussed over my scraped skin, gave me an extra dose of Tonic, and cautioned me to keep as healthy as possible.

Now, thinking back, I wondered if Abigail remembered that afternoon, too? We spoke of it only once after, wondering at the sign-carrying people, and then not at all because . . . she forgot.

"Pleasant thoughts?" Elizabeth asked now, pulling me back to this morning.

I nodded and closed my memories away, saving them for later.

"Yes," I said, making the word shorter than it was, and went into my morning shower.

6

In the bathroom, several females stood in front of mirrors, brushing their teeth. A couple of showers ran. So I wouldn't be the only one late.

Abigail and I were called into Principal Harrison's office after the wall incident.

He looked huge up close. I wanted to squint or cover my eyes. I kept thinking, *He's our pal. A principal is our pal.*

Trouble happens when people get close, Principal Harrison had said that day from behind his desk.

"You're crossing boundaries we consider safe here at Haven Hospital and Halls." He did that mouth movement—showing all his teeth, his lips curling up up up—then tapped his ballpoint pen on the cherry desk.

I had nodded, trying not to let the look on his face make me uncomfortable, but Abigail sat without moving, like she waited for something.

"As Terminals," Principal Harrison said, "we need to keep you varied as far as acquaintances go. Terminals don't have time to waste, do you?"

I shook my head.

Abigail sat there.

"So here it is: If you are not obedient—" Principal Harrison tapped on the desk again, his face that grotesque contortion. "—we take matters into our own hands. I've warned you."

Something cool slid over my skin.

He looked at both Abigail and me. I wasn't sure what to do, but Abigail said, "What are you saying, Principal Harrison?"

This principal was our friend.

He set the pen aside and clasped his hands. He leaned closer to us. "We'll send one of you away. Get rid of you." He paused. "Do you want that?"

I shook my head no. My hands trembled.

The principal is your pal. Your pal. Pal.

Principal Harrison cleared his throat.

I said, "I'll do better."

"That's what I told them," Principal Harrison said, "the counselors, your Teachers, Dr. King." He put his hands on his chest like our being here caused him pain. "You're Terminals." He was quiet then. Like that was all the answer we needed, and I guess it was. "We'll be increasing your Tonic. You may experience intensified dizziness and diarrhea for the first few days. Be consistent with the medicine and those side effects will ease."

"Are you saying," Abigail said, "that we can't spend as much time together because—?"

Principal Harrison cut her off. "It's already hard enough as it is, you watching your roommates change. Maybe not come back. This is for your own good. We don't want to do a big move, because so much is involved. But we will, if you keep doing these kinds of activities."

Words wouldn't come, but Abigail, who was recently full of words (and ideas, like looking over walls), spoke up. "Maybe being together makes us healthier," she said. "I feel better when I'm with Shiloh."

Principal Harrison opened a file. The kind that he brought into the dining room when someone leaves. "Push me, Abigail. See how fast we move you from Haven Hospital and Halls to another Terminal residence in another part of the country." The conversation, I could hear in his voice, was over. "Remember the rules. No more exploring. No more late nights. No more disobedience."

"Wait," I said. "Don't break the rules. I understand that. But if we continue to do things together—"

"More than any Terminal should . . . ," Principal Harrison said. He stood. Straightened his tie.

"Then you'll send one of us away?"

Principal Harrison pointed at the door. "I'm glad to see you understand. You're excused." He walked out of the room, past the walls lined with bookshelves, huge vases full of fresh flowers, and the big picture window that looked out on the yards covered in roses and summer flowers, benches and fountains.

I rubbed my eyes at the memory. Now, all around me, the voices of female Terminals echoed. Someone flushed a toilet. *I miss being able to explore with Abigail,* I wanted to say to the bathroom ceiling.

But saying it, admitting it, meant first, separation. Then Isolation. And finally, one of us being transferred from this unit to another. Or . . .

. . . or worse.

I didn't want to think about this.

I hung my robe and towel on a hook in the cleansing area and slipped my clothes off. I put my pajamas in the Room 18 bin, then stepped into the shower stall.

Hot water spilled over my shoulders when I walked under the faucet head. I tilted my face under the warmth, trying to erase leftover bits of memory. I rubbed the bath puff filled with lavender soap all over.

Bubbles puddled on the tile before being pulled down the drain. Washing my whole body first, I let the water relax me, saving my right side for last. Like always.

Long after the staples were out, there had been pain. And even though the scar was pink and healing, there was sensitivity. I didn't touch where the incision had been. The cut ran below my armpit to the bottom of my rib cage.

"We're taking only one lung. Not two," the doctor had said, his face growing large in my mind. A mask came down over my mouth and nose and I saw someone's huge brown eyes looking at me.

"Count backwards from one hundred."

I struggled.

"She reminds me of my own daughter."

"Yes, yes."

There were too many people. Too many voices. Words slid together. So did faces. Too many eyes. Too many noses. I fought.

"No more," I said. My voice echoed. I turned into the pelting water. "No more, Shiloh."

No Terminal *ever* speaks of what happened when they went away, even with the tokens left behind by the Disease—what it took from them—an obvious memento. Maybe I was the only one who remembered details. But we all had evidence of the Illness.

The air grew steamy. Too much thinking meant the dream would haunt me again. I didn't want that.

If I was lucky, the water would cleanse everything that bothered me, leaving me with an empty mind.

A few clusters of females walked down the corridor toward Main Hall and breakfast as I hurried to dress. I tucked the shirt into my jeans, then ran my fingers through my hair, splattering drops of water on the dresser. I made no effort to tie the shoelaces. Later I might be sorry I wore no socks, but I was late and I didn't have the extra seconds. Elizabeth was right. The whole day would be messed up because I hadn't gotten out of bed on time.

"She thinks she's so smart," I said to my reflection, running the towel through my hair one last time. The curls bounced back into place. "She's almost always right."

I hurried to the dining room, my hair making my shirt damp in spots all the way to my waist.

We aren't allowed more than walking inside, so I concentrated on getting into breakfast as fast as I could without swinging into a faster clip.

"Shiloh." My name came at me in a whisper.

"What?" Two females in Main Hall looked back. One of them, Esther, called, "There's not going to be anything left to eat, Shiloh."

I waved them on. "I'm coming." I took a few more steps. There stood Gideon—*Gideon*—in a window alcove.

"Shiloh," he said again, his voice too loud. Heavy curtains the color of grape juice fell from the ceiling to the window seat. He was almost hidden in the folds of purple.

"You can't be here." Sweat broke out on my forehead.

"Shhh," he said.

What in the Terminal world was he doing? I walked to where he hid, hesitant. This could mean trouble for us both. If he were seen. If we were caught together.

"I'm not that far from the Main Hall." He gestured to where everyone converged. Only the slowest were still in the hall. Terminals who had had recent operations or weren't used to their wheelchairs.

"What are you doing? You know the rules. Do you want Isolation?" I closed my mouth tight. "Or have you just gotten *out* of Isolation?"

He didn't answer.

"I can't stand here chatting with you. I'll miss breakfast." I tried not to say it, but the words came anyway. "The most important meal of the day."

Gideon grabbed for me and I dodged him. Had he gone mad? Been infected with something? Had he caught what Isaac had? "Don't!"

Gideon raised a finger to his lips, then spoke past it. "I need to talk to you, Shiloh." He reached for me again, staying hidden. "Come closer. So the others won't see us."

We were alone in the corridor. I kept my hands tucked in my pockets. If I needed to, I wanted to be able to get away. "I'll come closer if you stop grabbing at me."

"You are so pretty, Shiloh."

A strange feeling ran through my chest. "What are you talking about?"

He looked at his feet, then up at me again. His voice was somehow different. "The way you look, your skin, your hair—"

"I have no idea what you mean, Gideon. We're going to get in huge trouble—"

"You're right," he said. "We have only a few moments."

My pulse beat in my wrists. "Keep hidden in the curtains," I said. "I don't want to go to Isolation again." Nothing to do there but lie on the floor with my pain, and the white walls of the room. And the lights. It felt like I had been stored in a too-bright, empty closet.

"I'll be quick." He folded himself deeper in the drapes.

I moved a foot nearer, ready to run. Male Terminals can spread

45

Disease to female Terminals just like that. It's a proven scientific fact. And the reason we sit in different parts of the classrooms, lunchroom, and have recess in different parts of the yard. Why would Gideon risk this when his roommate was gone? When Isaac might not come back? The Disease could conquer him next.

And what did he mean, I was pretty? "Tell me whatever you have to," I said, itching to go. "I want to get to breakfast."

"Promise that you'll think over whatever I say to you."

If anyone saw me standing here, would they call for help?

I crossed my arms. "Think about what?"

"My plan."

I didn't answer.

"To save us."

What?

"To save all Terminals."

I tried to speak past my closed-up throat.

"Promise." There was that voice again.

I nodded.

"We're figuring things out," Gideon said. He spoke too slow. "We need your help. We need your memory. We need *you*."

My throat felt even tighter. I might never talk again. Or end up in the OR because my vocal cords didn't work anymore.

"We can talk more in Planting Committee if you sign up. Daniel will make sure you get in. We're starting seedlings for spring."

Outside the window, snow reflected the sun.

"It's too cold for Terminals to go outside."

"We have jackets. Ways to keep warm. And—"

The sharp sound of heels on marble echoed from down the hall.

Principal Harrison advanced on us. His face looked hard as concrete. I heard Gideon whisper from his hiding place, "Don't give me away."

My fingertips grew icy from Gideon's words.

"Ms. Shiloh," Principal Harrison said, closing the distance between us. "*You* are late." A few more steps and I could have touched his vest. I looked up at him. "This is the Terminal's most important meal of the day." His lips turned up, showing his teeth. He reminded me of a jackal I once saw on *Wild Terminal Kingdom.* "And *you* are missing it. You know the rules."

I nodded, wanting to peek back at the curtains. Somehow I didn't let myself. Instead, I kept my eyes on Principal Harrison's thin mustache.

"Yes, sir," I said. "I got a late start this morning. Elizabeth said this would throw off the whole day. She was right." Would he see I was lying? Send me to the Isolation Room?

I wasn't lying. Not really. I was omitting.

Tell on Gideon, a part of my brain said. *Report him. He's in the wrong place. He shouldn't be in the Females' Hallway. He shouldn't have a plan. Tell.*

The memory of someone hunched in the snow, that flashing light, popped into my head, made me pause. Had *that* been Gideon? I opened my mouth to speak.

"Do you have something to report?" Principal Harrison took a step closer. His eyebrows tried to meet over his nose.

Confess. All good Terminals are obedient. Stop the Disease by telling.

"I didn't . . ." The words came out garbled. I cleared my throat. "I didn't sleep so well last night."

Principal Harrison clapped his hands together. "An easy cure, Ms. Shiloh," he said. "You know that. After breakfast go to Infirmary. I'll make sure you have a sleeping aid waiting for you for tonight when you go to bed. Take it with your Tonic. There is no reason not to get your sleep."

He raised his meaty hand, then pointed down the hallway. "Get going."

"Yes, sir," I said. I felt dizzy, my skin prickly like blunt needles tapped all over, looking for a way into my flesh.

"What is it, Ms. Shiloh?"

"Sir?"

"You're hesitating. I said get to breakfast."

You have a chance. A second chance. You could be a hero. You could save the Terminals. Tell on Gideon right now.

I thought of Principal Harrison threatening to separate me and Abigail. I thought of the Isolation Room. Then took one step, and another, not sure how my feet even moved. I never wanted to be away from Abigail. Not for anything.

Speed up. Get in to breakfast. But I was afraid for Gideon.

"Do you need an escort?"

"Yes, sir. Please." I nodded.

"Then let's go. I have many Terminals to look after, you know. Not just you."

"Yes, sir."

At the cafeteria doors. I heard the soft voices of the Terminals.

"You Terminals are so slow," Principal Harrison said. "Hurry, unless you want me to lead you over to the breakfast line?"

I looked back over my shoulder, down the long hall. It was empty.

"No, sir," I said. "I can do it. Thank you for walking me here. I was light-headed." The complete truth. Even at this moment I couldn't believe I had broken one of the biggest rules of all at Haven Hospital & Halls.

Met with someone of the opposite gender.

What was Gideon thinking? What was *I* thinking? As I took a

bowl of cracked wheat cereal sprinkled with blueberries and driz-
zled with honey and cream, I knew I would stop at the Infirmary
for a sleeping aid. Perhaps a good night's sleep *would* make me feel
better.

7

Planting Committee met in the greenhouse office. This building
was situated on the west side of campus. That's what Ms. Iverson
said, when I asked her if I could sign up. The whole time I
thought, *Why do this?* Snowy weather can kill a Terminal. Plus, I
shouldn't meet with Gideon. Still, my mouth kept moving, asking
when and where and what time I should show up for the Planting
Committee.

"They need all the help they can get over there," Ms. Iverson said.
She nodded. "Dr. King says they'll put plants in the ground before
you know it. They're working on some hydroponics stuff. Do you
know what that is, Shiloh?"

I thought for a second, guilt crawling all over my skin. "Growing
with water only?"

"Right! Good for you. I'll get this turned in." Ms. Iverson filled
out paperwork on a clipboard. She held it against her chest. "You
know, I've never seen the kind of vegetables grown here. They're huge
and beautiful." She looked at me. "Perfect for nutrition and keeping
Terminals safe and cared for." More nodding. I sure was glad she
didn't do that in class. I'd never be able to concentrate.

Later that afternoon I stood at the double doors, looking outside across the grounds toward the greenhouses. The sun, brilliant and glittering off the snow, seemed full of spring.

What was it that Abigail had said? Spring meant a promise to her. Almost spring. Almost a promise.

And Gideon telling us we should be responsible for ourselves. Who would have thought that? Terminals responsible for finding cures and discovering what was wrong with us.

I zipped my jacket, tucked a scarf around my neck, then slipped into the breezy weather. Hurrying, I followed footprints and tire tracks across the snow.

Ahead, the wind whooshed around the corner of a closed-off building, pushing snowflakes ahead of it, twisting into a zephyr, then swishing away until the little tornado dissolved.

Hands deep in my pockets, I hunched tighter against the gusts of cold air. To the door marked OFFICE at the far end of the greenhouses. The place was empty except for a table and chairs, a desk (the Teacher's), and a whiteboard covered in writing. The room smelled of dirt and flowers, but I saw no plants in here. A side door swung open and Gideon came in, brushing his hair off his forehead with a gloved hand.

He said, "Glad you decided to join us, Shiloh." He lifted his chin to me. His voice softened. "I didn't think you'd show."

"You asked me to come."

"You're right." Gideon pulled out a chair and gestured for me to sit.

"The committee will be supportive. We needed someone to take Isaac's place. Lots to do around here."

"Wait. I'm Isaac's replacement? I hadn't realized that." Did that mean he wasn't coming back? The news made me uncomfortable. I wanted to leave.

Gideon didn't stop talking. "As an introduction, there's lots to get done for spring—planting seedlings and starts, fertilizing, working the grounds."

My eye twitched. "I shouldn't be here with you alone. It's against the rules. I think I should go back."

Gideon checked the chart. "And when I said you're pretty, what I meant is, it's nice to look at you. I like you, Shiloh."

I wasn't sure what to do, so I stood there, my weight on one foot. "I don't think you should tell me that."

"I know I shouldn't. We're not allowed."

"Please," I said. I should go. But the disobedient part of me wanted to hear more.

"Sorry." Gideon dipped his head, looked up at me through his eyelashes. "I'll do better." His face colored, like maybe he had a fever. "You already know this, Shiloh, but many Terminals make light work."

"I understand." I didn't need a reminder from a Terminal like Gideon. He didn't follow rule one. Then he spoke inappropriate words, making me want to hear him say these things again.

"There are supposed to be Teachers here," I said, raising my voice. My head pounded with the volume, so I lowered my tone. "We can't be in here without direction."

"I won't tell you my feelings again. Unless you want me to."

I took a step back and bumped into the doorjamb. "I'll never want that," I said. "Terminals spread Disease—"

We both stood quiet. Gideon pointed at the whiteboard. "There's our direction. A list of things they want done. We won't be alone. Ms. Iverson or Mr. Tremmel or someone else will come to the greenhouses to check on us. We don't stay in here but work where we're needed."

"All right," I said, unsure. I sat down. Did Gideon tell me the truth? There was dirt on the surface of the tabletop and I dusted a clean space to rest my hands.

The side door opened and Daniel wheeled himself over near Gideon. I could see rows upon rows of tiny plants in the huge room that he came from.

Daniel didn't acknowledge me. *He* knew how Terminals should act. He tucked his hair behind his ears. There was grime under his nails.

I felt jittery. Lopsided almost, like I had after the operation. Now there were two males and only one me.

"We're waiting for another," Gideon said. He stared straight into my eyes. I looked away. *It's nice to look at you.* What was it with this Terminal? "Daniel, you know Shiloh, right?"

"Sure," Daniel said.

The door to outside burst open and cold air pushed into the room. Abigail rushed in, head covered against the cold. "Sorry I'm late."

I couldn't think of anything to say, and then, "Abigail. Since when?"

She slipped into a chair and scooted up to the table in the seat next to mine. "Didn't expect me, did you?" she asked.

"No."

Why hadn't she told me about Planting Committee? I thought we talked about everything. Would she read my thoughts and answer? But she just gazed at the tabletop once she settled in her seat.

"I wanted to talk about this spring's planting," Gideon said. "It'll only take a couple of minutes. Then you can get on with whatever else you have to do."

"I have to read *Lord of the Flies*," Abigail said, like she didn't owe me an explanation. "I still haven't written that paper on why Piggy deserved to die."

"Do you have the planting sheets, Daniel?" Gideon asked.

"Yes." Daniel dug around in a bag attached to his wheelchair, then handed a thin folder to Gideon. "I've logged that we've put in peas and spinach and onions already. There are Terminals working with the cold frames. Seedlings have been planted, as you know, and the . . ."

Rubbing my palm in the bits of leftover soil, I wondered at Abigail. She gawked at Daniel. Her mouth looked funny. Her cheeks, rosy.

Too many pink-faced Terminals in this room.

What was so interesting about Daniel anyway? He looked like everyone else though he was big enough, I bet, to play soccer or football, or maybe even rugby, games we've seen the Whole play on *Incredible Sports Disasters*. Even with his legs missing, Daniel was wider than lots of the male Teachers. Strong arms, thick neck. If he lived long enough, he would be a huge adult.

Why would Abigail concentrate on a male like that?

"Is there something you want to add to the list, Shiloh?" Daniel asked.

What did he want to know? I cleared my throat.

"If there's anyone who knows about food," Abigail said, "it's Shiloh. Don't you?"

A heater kicked on and warm air pushed the cold away.

"I love to eat, if that's what you mean."

"All Terminals do," Gideon said.

Now Gideon, Daniel, *and* Abigail waited for me to answer. My stomach turned. I pushed away from the table. "I like everything."

"How are the dreams?" Gideon asked.

It felt like the world rotated in slow motion. Abigail's eyebrows were raised.

It's inappropriate to mention the dreams. They're private.

"I don't dream that often." The lie coursed through me, large enough it could have filled the room. I racked my brain for food references from *Of Mice and Men,* the book I had just read. All I

53

could think of was rabbits. "I've heard of blue potatoes. They're native to South America. Could we try that? Or amaranth? It's a grain."

Daniel wrote.

"Jicama?" I said. "Tomatillos?"

Something touched my ankle and I jumped, my stomach flipping.

"Excuse me," Gideon said. "What about tangelos? We have the tangerine trees already, and the orange and grapefruit trees. We could start something new." He scooted closer to the table, bumping into me again. Why was he such a klutz? I wanted him to stop. Now. He made me sick.

Again the outside door opened and this time Ms. Iverson came into the room. "It's freezing out there. Sorry to be late." She hurried to the desk. Relief flooded my body. It seemed my lung trembled as I pulled oxygen in. All I needed was to be obedient, I thought, licking my lips. "You finishing up the lists?" Ms. Iverson asked.

Gideon nodded.

"Dr. King wants something floral-ish. Maybe edible flowers? That's what he says in a note he sent me today." She addressed me. "Dr. King keeps the flowers in abundance here as a memory of his wife and child."

"Put that on the list," Gideon said, and Daniel wrote it down.

"Miss Maria said food with color. Like chocolate peppers and purple cabbage, things like that. Anyway, I'm here to send you back to the building for dinner. And to collect the paperwork, so get going—"

A bell sounded from across campus. "See?" she said, like Ms. Iverson had made the bell ring. "I'll get the rest of the Terminals from the greenhouses and send them in. You run along."

Good. I wanted to get out of here as fast as possible. But Gideon was quicker, pushing Daniel ahead of me.

"Shiloh, wait," Abigail said, but I didn't slow my step.

She came up next to me just as Daniel peered over his shoulder to where I walked and then back again to Gideon. Daniel seemed different, though I couldn't say why. His mouth turned down and his eyebrows were knit together. He acted as though *I* had done something offensive.

"Leave her alone, Daniel," Abigail said. She walked close to me. Her mouth moved in that upward curve, and it spread across her face, making her eyes shine even though there wasn't much light left in the graying sky.

Now *she* was doing it. That unnatural look. When had she started contorting her face in that terrible way? What was it with everyone? "I'm so glad you're here, Shiloh," Abigail said. "I hoped you'd say yes."

While the stretched-out lips and the teeth showing in such a big way was uncomfortable to see on Abigail, when she spoke, the voice was her voice and it calmed me.

"You should have told me," I said, pulling in tight under my jacket. "You know we shouldn't meet with males alone. And who keeps track of us? The whole thing makes me nervous."

Evening settled over the grounds, making the world glow-in-the-dark blue. Ahead of us the Main Building lights twinkled in the early dusk.

"When I thought you'd be ready, I invited you," Abigail said.

I stopped in the cold, shivering. "No. You sent Gideon." She was silent. "You didn't tell me, Abigail. And we always do things together."

There was that mouth thing. "Will you forgive me? Now that we're on the same team?"

I shook my head. "Stop with the face contortions."

"Oh, the smiling? I'll work on it. But when it's just you and me or you and me and Daniel and Gideon, well, I may not be able to stop. Now, let's go. I'm starving." Abigail's words were a whispery cloud. She tossed her hair over her shoulder.

We walked on, snow quiet.

"How long have you been coming out here?"

"A couple months. You were working kitchen duty."

"Okay." *Okay* was the wrong word. "Why didn't you tell me?"

Abigail stopped, kicked at the ground, then said, "Gideon asked when Isaac left who I would choose. I said you." The cold bit at my face. "Listen to him, Shiloh. He can save us. I know it."

Her lips didn't move. Her words were a dream. Another dream I shouldn't have.

Then she was off, leaving me in the yard. I stood there, frozen from more than the weather. Watched her stop to say something to Gideon, who appeared in the doorway and looked over to where I stood. A wind came from the south, a little warmer. I trudged on, closer and closer to where Gideon waited with the door open. A few Terminals walked from other parts of outside into the building for dinner. There was little noise other than the wind.

Why was I so unsettled? Why did I feel so left out?

I slowed, leaving dragging footprints behind in the snow.

"Are you coming?" Gideon asked, his voice hushed. I couldn't see his expression. The hall light spilled out around him. Making him a shadow. Haloing his head.

A black shadow. Hunched over. Running to the gazebo.

My heart quickened. "Yes," I said.

My face felt like plastic, fake, as though it wasn't my own. As though it belonged to someone else.

Gideon swung the door wide. I passed him and hurried into the stone entry. He brushed close enough for me to feel his breath, warm, on my skin.

"Sorry about Daniel. He's moody."

Moody?

What was this with everyone in this group? What was wrong with them all? I wanted to run. To leap away. All my nerves screamed for me to go.

Gideon held me back, grabbing for my arm, then clasping his cold hand on mine. For a second I thought I might vomit. I jerked away, clamped a hand over my mouth.

"Meet me tonight, Shiloh," he said, his voice low. "Meet me right here. We have things to talk about."

"What are you doing?" I pulled in the cold outside air, trying to quiet my nausea. Then I got right in Gideon's face even though the nearness made me gag. "Every time you touch me, I get sick to my stomach. You say things that are wrong. At least keep your hands off me."

He nodded. "I can take care of that," he said. "The nausea. The dreams. The obedience. I can tell you how to feel human. Meet me here, tonight. Midnight."

The desire to run slammed through me. It was a part of my cells. I must be a good Terminal. An obedient Terminal.

"I'm not listening to you," I said, and pushed past him, doing all I could not to shake as I walked away.

I am not even asleep when I see him.

He slinks in the room, slides across the floor, nothing but a shadow.

Come on, Shiloh.

Come with me.

You're nice to look at and I can help you with this.

He sweeps his hand around and I see all my roommates. They are quiet. Dreamless.

Only Abigail's eyes are open. Unblinking.

She watches from her bed. Not moving. Eyes glittering.

Come on.

We'll leave.

Cure the Terminals.

Give our lives.

Take your breath.

He leans over my bed. His mouth is on mine. Soft. Warm. My stomach twists. He presses closer.

Is all over me. Then sucks the air out of my lung and I am empty of my life.

8

I awoke, heart slamming against my ribs. It felt as though someone still pressed against me. I was sure I would die. Only the early-morning light seeping through the window convinced me I might be all right. My mouth was too dry. All the females slept. Abigail's hair snaked off her pillow.

I lay in bed for a long time. The next time I opened my eyes, Abigail was gone, Elizabeth was getting up, and Mary had gone in to shower. My dream stayed with me, a haunting.

In the dining room, I reasoned there are worse ways to die than having your breath sucked from you. Like being eaten away until there was nothing left. Dying like many of the Terminals did, piece by piece.

Abigail's chair was empty.

I sat down. Lined up the large spoon, small spoon, fork, and knife. Setting out my plate of food. Where was she?

Being assaulted by Gideon? Maybe he made it a habit to attack females, leaping out of curtains. No, he was here, across the room. He sent me a slight nod, one I almost couldn't see.

Instead of acknowledging him, I set to eating my whole-wheat pancakes with mango sauce and fresh strawberries. I'd taken extra turkey bacon. Eating more might ease the queasiness in my stomach. I drank some cranberry juice and was contemplating seconds when Abigail came into the dining room, head bent, hair forward.

Some of the Teachers watched her. There was a bad taste on the back of my tongue.

Abigail dropped into her chair.

"Where have you been?"

"I slept in," she said.

I blinked at her lie. "That's not true. You were gone before I even got up."

Abigail wouldn't look at me, and right then I knew. *She* had met with Gideon last night. Without another word, she trotted off before the breakfast line closed down. Miss Maria waved Abigail over, fingers motioning in the air.

Worry settled in my bones. He couldn't get me, so Gideon got her. I wouldn't be able to eat this bacon after all. And no seconds either, no matter how good it tasted.

"What have you done?" I asked as soon as Abigail sat back down.

She looked up from her plate. "What do you mean?"

59

"You know what I mean." My voice came out more harsh than I meant.

Esther looked over at us. "Arguing? Terminals never argue."

"No, we're not," I said. "We're discussing."

Abigail popped a strawberry in her mouth. She was so casual, she confused me. Did I imagine this? Maybe I didn't remember as well as I thought. Maybe I hadn't heard Gideon. Last night seemed distant. Almost part of my dream. I couldn't quite tell the two events apart.

The dining room hummed with the low sound of voices. Ms. Iverson made a movement for Abigail to hurry. Mr. Tremmel carried his tray back to the kitchen, then left with a few males.

Esther and Martha headed off to class. The space near us cleared out, giving me the chance to speak.

"You were with him," I said.

Abigail just chewed.

"Weren't you? Last night."

"With whom?"

"You know what I'm talking about, Abigail." The room felt too warm.

"Let's go, girls," Ms. Iverson said. "We've got lots to do in class today."

I pretended I didn't hear our Teacher, though my body wanted to respond, to put away my tray, get ready to learn, do what I was supposed to do.

I swallowed the obedience.

"What are you thinking? You know the rules. And you know the consequences."

Abigail shrugged. She lifted her chin a little. She wasn't even ashamed. She didn't even care that she'd broken the rules.

"I wasn't with Gideon," she said. She sighed. "Look, Shiloh, it's okay. I promise." She shifted closer in her chair. "I'm not the same as before."

I couldn't speak.

"I'm different. Changed."

"Ill?" The word came out strangled.

"New."

"I don't want to hear this." I put my hands on my ears, but Abigail had stopped talking and just ate.

"Abigail. Shiloh. Time to go." Ms. Iverson motioned for us to follow.

Again I fought to not obey, but my body stood.

"You have to listen." Abigail's face went from her normal, calm appearance to one that made my legs feel weak. It was like she had never meant anything more than whatever she might say right now.

I tried to cover my ears again and gather my breakfast things, both at the same time. Only those who couldn't leave the room without assistance remained.

Ms. Iverson called from the doorway, "Eat in a hurry, Abigail. You have to get your nourishment before studies begin."

"Listen, Shiloh." Abigail's voice was urgent. "Trust Gideon."

"What?" The glass toppled from my tray and fell to the floor, shattering. Cranberry juice spread like blood. I knelt to pick up the bigger shards of glass. "Why do you have so much faith in him?"

"He knows things, Shiloh," Abigail said. "He has connections."

"I have no idea what you mean." I straightened. "There's no saving us."

Ms. Iverson came over. How had she gotten to my side so quick? "Go to class, Shiloh. The Staff will clean up."

"Yes, ma'am." I didn't even look back when I left the room.

———

Images of documentaries I'd seen in history played in my head. Jonestown, Waco, Heaven's Gate. There was that whole city not too far from here. All those Terminals gone. Terminals annihilated because they broke free of the school, went into society, and were wiped out by the Whole who didn't think Terminals should mix with the free states. And not a thing was done to protect the Terminals.

All of them, murdered.

But

we were safe here.

I closed my eyes.

There were awful things that could happen to us. Yes, what our Illnesses caused. But other stuff, too. Annihilation. I remembered the pictures of the bodies, some facedown, bloated, bleeding, limbs missing on many. Not one had survived. Even the youngest were dead. Flies crawling in their eyes and opened mouths.

Haven Hospital & Halls kept Terminals from being murdered.

I remembered the crowds, the picketing on the other side of the wall.

Did they want us gone, too? Want us dead? Annihilated?

It only made sense they did. Dr. King told us often that the world doesn't understand Terminals, that we're protected by Haven Hospital & Halls. That this place is what we call it, a haven from an angry, uneducated world.

I hurried, breaking another rule, leaving Abigail in the lunchroom, the broken glass on the floor, knowing that disobedience was far worse than anything Abigail or Gideon or Daniel could imagine.

"I waited for you."

The voice came from the curtains. Too familiar, even with me only hearing it once before. Too dangerous.

"You didn't show up."

I stopped but didn't look at the curtains.

"I'm not interested," I said. "I don't care what you have to say." I clenched my hands so that I felt my nails in my palms. I hated this lie. Because I *was* interested. I *was*. And that caused the blood to rush through me, pounding in my ears.

"It's for you, Shiloh. Abigail wants you to have the gift of knowing." Gideon's voice sounded like syrup tastes. "All you have to do is listen. All you have to do is see." He hesitated and then said, "And I want it for you, too. I want you to be with us."

"I *never* want to be with you."

"I understand." There was a longer pause before Gideon spoke again. "But ask yourself a few questions, Shiloh. Why do we all dream like we do? Why isn't the outside world allowed in? Why aren't we allowed out?"

"We'll die if—"

"I know *their* answers." Gideon's attitude was the same as when he had thrown the chair. Hostile. "I want answers for *us*. For Terminals. For you."

"We know why we're here," I said. My voice was insistent.

"You're *programmed* to know that, Shiloh. Think past class. Think past what you've been taught."

I swallowed. "I can't." I felt the fight in my muscles. I must follow. I must obey. I must not listen to anything that was against our belief system.

"Daniel told her you wouldn't do it," he said. "Abigail begged that we include you. She said there's a part of you that wants to be free of here."

Something moved in my chest, an unfamiliar part of the struggle. Join them because Daniel said I wouldn't? I looked away from the curtains. Down the hall I could see the massive fireplace. The chairs where I sometimes went to read.

"He was right," I said.

Walk on, I thought. *Go.* But I stood still.

Abigail thought there was a part of me that wanted something different.

"If you change your mind," Gideon said, "meet us at the entrance to the kitchen. Twelve thirty tonight. Don't drink the Tonic and you'll stay awake."

I marched off down the hall, to my room, where I threw myself on my bed to think. The covers smelled clean. I knew I'd miss class and end up with another dose of Tonic and maybe one-on-one time with Principal Harrison. But I stayed in bed anyway.

That night, the Tonic sat on my bedside table like every night. This is part of Miss Maria's duty. But I'd never thought of it. Just swallowed the bright red liquid, made with acai juice, to keep myself as healthy as possible. I didn't ask questions.

Ever.

Thick liquid, sweet, with a bitter aftertaste. Never wondered what the Tonic was for. They told me. I believed. I felt irritated with myself. Food was important to me. Why not the Tonic?

It was habit.

If you had bad dreams, you got an extra bit of Tonic. Why? You needed your sleep.

If you were dizzy when another Terminal got near you, you had to make sure to down that extra drink. Why? To keep you from spreading germs.

Tonic was a directive.

Ask for more if you needed something to settle your stomach.

Terminals could transfer sickness—don't get too close. The Tonic builds your immunities from being near someone, especially some-one of the opposite gender. Stay away from the opposite gender.

I slipped out of my clothes and put on pajamas, crumpling the blue jeans I'd worn, then tossing the dirty clothes in the laundry bas-ket. Tomorrow morning, those clothes would be on top of my dresser for me to put away, or hanging in my closet. Who did that? And how did they keep my things separate from everyone else's?

I'd never wondered.

But tonight was different.

I was different. (Like when Abigail said she was changed?)

My differences made me creep around at night. Lie awake later than the others. Made me remember what I wanted to forget.

Tonight I was different because of Gideon's actions. *He* had tempted Abigail somehow. And that changed me.

Tonight, my roommates spoke in whispers. Brahms played. I yawned.

Why did I give Gideon so much control? Why was I even think-ing of him?

"Drink your Tonic, Shiloh," I said, looking into the cup.

The lights dimmed.

Sure, I thought Gideon's speech had merit. I wanted Terminals to get better. Not lose parts. Not die. But Gideon was *breaking* rules. And if we wanted to get free, we had to *follow* the rules. And his words to me. That he *liked* to look at me. Something burned in my skin.

I swirled the Tonic.

This was why Terminals should stay away from each other. Close association caused anxiety. I could see that. Feel it, too. Whenever I stood side by side with a Terminal, especially a male (which I never did unless it was necessary). When I looked at Gideon. Saw him across the room from me.

I tilted the Tonic toward my lips, tasted the sweetness.

"Good night, everyone," Elizabeth said.

"Night," Mary said.

"I hope you sleep better." Abigail sat up in her bed, watching me.

Wait.

If Gideon was right, and Terminals had to do it themselves, *for* themselves, *should* they follow rules?

"You okay?" Abigail asked. I ignored her.

"I need to use the restroom," I said, mumbling. Confused, I went into the hall and down to the lavatory. The little cup bent in my hand. The liquid jiggled with each step.

The light came on when I walked into the tiled room. I saw myself in the mirror. My eyes looked too big. My hair seemed too wild. There was red on my top lip.

"Drink it," I whispered to my reflection.

I went in a stall. Sat down. Tossed the Tonic back. No! I jumped up, spun around, and spit the whole mouthful into the toilet, flushing the red away. I went to the sink and washed my mouth out, twice.

Blood rushed to my face.

"What have I done?" I said. I was crazy! Disobedient! Putting myself at risk!

"It's just to see." I rested my forehead against my image's forehead.

Or . . . or (should I even think it?) this was to find a cure.

I let out a whimper. "Right." My voice sounded like I stood in a soup can. "You're finding a cure in the john."

I washed my hands, then splashed cool water on my face.

"Are you okay, Shiloh?" Abigail slid from the darkened doorway into the light.

"What are you doing here?" Had she seen me? Did she know what I had done?

Abigail's lips trembled. "Just checking on you," she said. Her voice was quiet. "I didn't mean to offend."

The room smelled like soap. Who kept this place so clean?

"You do offend, Abigail. I don't even recognize you," I said, my mouth taking over. "You won't let *me* make the decision. Let *me* have a choice. You do things without me, never telling me you're going to." I pushed past her, hearing the toilet flush again as I went down the hall. Once I was in our room, I crawled in bed, turning my back to her when Abigail got into her own bed and whispered over to me, "Sorry."

HAVEN
HOSPITAL & HALLS
Where You Matter
Established 2020

Note to all Staff

Please Watch For:
Change in food consumption
Students being too sleepy or too alert
Sudden mood changes
Laughter
Uncommon sickness (i.e., headache, diarrhea, sweating, shakiness)

Any and all of these (and similar) behaviors MUST be reported to school officials immediately.

9

I couldn't sleep.

Maybe it was because the night music had stopped or because I flushed the evening Tonic or because I was nervous I would miss the twelve thirty rendezvous. After Brahms ended, the bedroom filled with the sounds of sleeping.

Those nighttime sighs, the late hour, and going to bed at 10:00 P.M. made my eyes heavy. Maybe this one time I would sleep without wanting to, instead of lying awake.

The clock over the fireplace mantel called out the half hour. It had never seemed so loud. Now the tock seemed to boom. How did I not notice it? Or sleep through it? There was the rush of a spring wind blowing around the building, whistling in at what must be a small crack in the window. There was the settling of the beds when someone rolled over and the soft footsteps of Ms. Iverson, who checked rooms before she headed to her own room. Funny how I had never heard her walking on the wooden hall floors before tonight.

And then there were the voices of men, talking about cleaning.

A cleaning crew. I had a vague recollection of a group of individuals (were they Terminal or Whole? I didn't know) who I sort of heard other late nights.

I blinked, eyes hot.

Keep awake.

Did this group do the laundry, too?

I flopped over and stared at the ceiling.

Sleep, my mind told me. *You need your rest. Disobedience equals death.*

I couldn't believe I would run the risk of Isolation—and all for Abigail.

I was sure Gideon had beguiled her. Like Jim Jones had deceived the residents of Jonestown and convinced them to commit suicide. Or how the People had turned against the innocent during the Terminal Massacres.

Tonight I would break the rules and convince Abigail not to follow Gideon. I would convince them both.

The clock donging twelve times jarred me awake. I sat, sick to my stomach. I had slept and not meant to.

After throwing off the covers, I moved on tiptoe from my bed. To the dresser. Put on sweats. Sweatshirt. A rubber band to pull my hair back. Socks. No shoes.

I went to the window.

What was left of the snow glowed. But there was no one out there. I mean, Gideon wasn't out there. The night was still.

Sneaking to the door, I peered down the hall. The clock said it was 12:10. 12:10! Still another twenty minutes to wait. No wonder Abigail was late for breakfast this morning. She'd been exhausted.

I walked back to my bed and sat down. Closed my eyes. Opened them. Hummed. Recited the Pledge three times. "We are one. All colors make up who we are. We are the same. The Terminal. We help the Whole. We benefit the World. We will make a difference."

We will make a difference.

Like Gideon said.

I propped myself in the sitting position and leaned against the headboard. I would close my eyes to the count of three. It wouldn't hurt.

Not even five minutes later Gideon spoke. "Shiloh. You're late."

I awoke. Gideon stood in the doorway, a dark silhouette.

"Are you meeting with me and Abigail or not? We've been waiting for you. Every second out in view puts us at risk."

"I'm coming," I said. I'd show him. Tell them both how I felt.

"Hurry," Gideon said. He pressed his finger to his lips. Motioned with his head and said, "People are working. Ms. Iverson is up with the cleaning crew." Then he was gone, slipping away like a ghost.

"Gideon." I kept my voice soft. The sound caught in the walls, in the curtains, in other Terminals' sleeping quarters. I hurried along faster than normal. My sweatshirt made me so hot, I wondered if I could bear it. I flapped the front, letting cool air up against my skin.

If you go outside, you'll be cold, I thought. *If you sneak to the gazebo.* Go to the wall. Peek over. The people with signs, eyes bloodred, flashed in my memory.

No, I *wouldn't* sneak to the gazebo, wouldn't climb the wall. I would follow the rules, except this once, and I would fix what was broken with Abigail and Gideon. I would convince them meetings like this were wrong. I would tell Abigail not to trust that Gideon could save any Terminal at all. Logic told me that was impossible. It should tell her the same thing.

He rounded the corner up ahead.

I ran after him. "Gideon," I called. My voice echoed. Why was it so loud? "I want to talk to you."

"Shhh," he said. "Shhh, Shiloh. They'll hear us."

At last, I caught up with him. His back was to me. His hair looked green in the light of the EXIT sign. I grabbed his shoulder, pulled hard to turn him around, my stomach somersaulting. I would tell him how I felt about Abigail being with him at night. Before we got to her.

His whole arm and a chunk of his shoulder came off in my hand. Blood sprayed in the air, splashed on the floor. I felt it, warm, under my feet. Felt the blood run over my fingers, down my hand.

"Look what you did, Shiloh," Gideon said. He shook his head at me, his eyes glowing. "How can I save the Terminals if I bleed out?"

His eyebrows disappeared. Then his mouth, nose, and eyes, and then his whole face was gone. There was nothing but a black hole where he had once been. His shoulder and arm were heavy in my hands. Warm. Wet. I dropped it to the floor. It hit the ground with a *thunk*.

"No."

The fingers reached for my ankle, then clawed at the floor, trying to get to me, but I stepped back.

"No!"

My own voice woke me, my eyes flying open.

It was another dream. A crazy, crazy dream. I clutched at the covers. Swallowed again and again. I should have taken the Tonic.

It took some time to not think of that arm coming loose. The way it had torn. The weight of it. I shivered. I could still see the hand reaching for me. Could feel the warmth of the blood on my feet.

I needed to go. Get this whole thing over with though the dream felt like a warning or an omen.

My head and stomach felt just like that, topsy-turvy, upside-down. I steadied myself by touching the bed. Then in slow motion I went to the door, so I could see the time.

Had I overslept?

It was 12:25.

Time to go.

If I had the courage.

I was sent to Isolation the morning after Abigail and I snuck to the kitchen.

I'd written a note on the whiteboard there, a poem about wanting more food and finding everything locked away.

Terminals need nourishment past sup
Give us something because we're up.

Abigail and I'd given each other the nod of approval, then headed out and done more exploring and, later, gone to bed.

The next day, when our teacher, Mrs. Galloway (who's been here forever and works with ten-year-olds), asked who had graffitied the whiteboard outside the kitchen, I didn't even hesitate. I confessed. I *felt* the urge to tell the truth and so I did. I spent twenty-four hours in Isolation, going out only for sips of water and to use the restroom.

I never told on myself again. Even when the urge to expose incidents turned fierce, I kept my mouth shut. If I had to bite confessions off, chew them up, and swallow them, I kept my bad behaviors to myself.

There was plenty to tell: nightmares, sneaking out, and now this running to meet a male.

I wouldn't confess saving Abigail and Gideon, either. There was no reason to make it hard on anyone.

But if it was necessary, I might disclose information on Gideon to save *him*. To stop him from ending up like Romeo, dead from staying in Isolation and having no water. Ever. It happened. We read that in books.

Isolation was its own nightmare: no bed to sleep on, no pillow or comforter, not even a place to use the restroom. Nothing to eat—*nothing!*—and little to drink. Then there was the steady whine of words that filled the mind and blocked out everything else, the stark walls and no one else at all.

If I had to, I would save Gideon from himself. Like Juliet tried to save Romeo and then died in the process.

I whispered the last line of *Romeo and Juliet,* "For never was a story of more woe/Than this of Juliet and defiant Romeo," and stepped into the hall. Ms. Iverson, I was sure, was long asleep. Still, I felt nervous. What if I found Gideon? What if his arm was gone? Or came off in my own hand?

My stomach tightened. Maybe if I counted. *Onetwothreefourfi*—

No! I could talk my way out of the worry.

"None of those things will happen, Shiloh," I said. "Please, please don't let that happen." I kept my voice quiet, but in the dark hall the words felt like they floated near the doorways, waiting for someone to follow behind and collect what I'd said.

Tonight, I was on my own and my dream did not help at all. In the shadowed corners, I saw that hole of a face. The curtains looked like Dr. King in his lab coat. A severed head swung near the ceiling. The fireplace seemed to yawn wide. I clutched my sweatshirt close and edged along the halls.

"What in the world are you doing, Shiloh?" I felt like a crazed Terminal. Tonight was nothing like exploring before. Tonight was dangerous.

I walked down the corridor to the open expanse of the great hall that connected all the wings of Haven Hospital & Halls.

And then I saw it.

Something real, not just my imagination. Ahead of me. I thought I might swallow my tongue. *Let this be another dream.* I squeezed my eyes shut. No arms. No shoulders. Why didn't I take the nighttime Tonic? I could be safe in bed, sleeping. What had I been thinking? . . .

I opened my eyes. Pulled in air. Squeezed my hands together. There it was again! Farther away this time.

Unable to move I stopped. If I had wanted, I'm not sure I could have gone on.

What should I do? I couldn't even answer my own question. What if I screamed? How would I explain what I was doing awake, fully dressed at this late hour if the Teacher on duty saw my offensive behavior? If I didn't move at all, maybe whatever that was wouldn't see me. I could go right back to bed. I *would* go back and—

The figure slunk away, moving with speed and with a low *shhhh* sound. The hair rose all over my body. A cold sweat broke out down my back and under my arms.

It turned the corner in the direction I was to go, then disappeared from my sight.

Move, Shiloh. But I couldn't. I was melted ice.

"Shiloh, are you coming?"

My voice came out a squeak. "Abigail? Please be real," I said. "Please don't let me break off your only arm."

"Break off my arm? What are you talking about?"

And there she was. Stepping out of the darkness.

"Are you okay?" Her voice was soft as the night. I felt my eyes burn, I was that relieved.

My legs were no longer tied to the floor. I could move, though my kneecaps felt like they might pop off.

"Abigail," I said. "Oh, Abigail. I'm so . . ." I couldn't think of a word to describe it, the way I felt, the nerves that ran through me. ". . . jumpy."

She came up close. "Come on. We've got work to do and I've got things to show you." She gestured and I followed her, relief warming the coldest parts of my body.

All around us the school seemed alive. Flickering shadows. Sounds, as though the walls breathed. I wanted to run, but I knew I'd not get far. Abigail slunk down the hall, making no noise at all. She blended in with the darkness. Were those shapes Terminals moving from corner to corner like Abigail did?

"I want to go back to bed, Abigail," I said. My mouth felt dry but words squeezed out. "This is bad. You know what will happen if our blood pressure goes up. We can be called out during lunch. Neither of us wants that."

Abigail didn't answer. Just kept walking. I had no choice but to follow—or go back to our room alone. Then, when would I tell her and Gideon to stop meeting? I might throw up right this second. Instead, I followed after Abigail, who seemed to know how to disappear into the night.

10

Abigail walked longer than forever. When I tried to talk to her, she shushed me. Down stairs, down more stairs, down we went. The hallways growing colder, then colder still, until far ahead I saw a thin strip of light, the color of warmth. Like a fire burning.

"We're almost there," Abigail said. Without warning, she came to a halt and I almost ran into her. My already upset stomach turned over and I had to think positive thoughts to keep what was left of dinner down.

"What is it?" I asked. What did she see? Someone coming to get us? The Thing?

Abigail faced me. "This is all going to sound unusual, Shiloh. What you hear tonight will make you feel as though you are deceitful." I heard her swallow. "But I want you to *really* listen."

I nodded even though I knew she couldn't see me that well. I was here to save *her*. I could listen to what Gideon had to say.

"Okay."

Abigail didn't move. My unsettled guts twisted.

"This could mean our lives, Shiloh. Yours and mine and Gideon's and . . ."

In the dark Abigail looked ghostlike, half there.

". . . and the rest of the Terminals."

An odd emotion bubbled up in my chest. "*He's* said that, Abigail," I said. I pulled courage from somewhere near my toes, where it had hidden, during the walk. "That doesn't mean anything."

Abigail said, "Promise me you'll listen. Promise me, Shiloh. With your head and heart. Promise to hear Gideon out."

Her tone, her intensity, alarmed me.

"Okay," I said. "I will."

She gave a quick nod. "Let's go."

I followed her though my body, my head (maybe even my heart—as she said?) didn't want to.

I heard the low mumble of voices.

Pain pounded behind my eyes.

"Ready?"

Nodding once, I followed her into a room so small, it wasn't more than a closet.

"Took you long enough." There was Daniel. I saw the tiny TV he stared at reflected in his glasses.

"You, too, Daniel?"

He sighed like he was tired of me already. "Yes, Shiloh. I'm here for the Cause. Just like you."

Pictures flashed through my head. Waco burning, smoke pluming into the sky. Photos of Terminals' parted-out bodies slumped in filth and squalor. Lines of families, dead. The Whole and Terminals alike had stood for causes. *With* causes. I shuddered.

"I passed you in the hallway," Daniel said. "Followed you awhile, then slid by. Made sure you didn't tell."

"How were *you* going to stop me? Run over me?" It felt like ants crawled around in my stomach.

Abigail let out a sound I had never heard anyone but the Teachers make. Her voice lilted up almost too high, the sharp sound cackling from her.

I covered my ears. "Stop!"

"She's laughing, Shiloh," Gideon said. "It's something you can't do, because of the Tonic."

"What are you talking about?"

Abigail leaned near me but I stepped away, bumping into the

desk. It was too hot in here and I felt ill at ease. The noise, the *laughing,* made me even more agitated. "We can laugh. We can smile." She made her face edge up, showing her teeth.

"Don't." I looked at the top of Daniel's head.

The walls moved closer. I'd find out what this was about first. *Then* I'd go.

"Don't check up on me anymore, Daniel," I said. I felt ruffled, like the wind had blown the wrong way through my hair.

"He's joking, Shiloh," Abigail said. "It's another thing that comes with the Tonic being out of your system. You can tease. Have fun."

Pressure overwhelmed me. I wanted to get away. *Concentrate.*

When I left, I would take Abigail with me. I didn't care what happened to Gideon and Daniel. Abigail and I would go and hope we never fell ill again.

"We can't afford any leaks," Daniel said, his voice gruff. "We can't be found out or we're all doomed."

"Doomed?" My shoulders were heavy, weighted. I made myself speak. "A bit dramatic, don't you think?"

Daniel looked at Gideon. "I told you bringing too many people would make problems for us. And another female? Why did it have to be another female?"

"What's wrong with females?" Abigail asked but didn't wait for an answer. "You know I wanted Shiloh here. She's my friend. I want her to leave with us."

Head spinning, I leaned against the wall, steadying myself.

Gideon almost stepped on Abigail's words. "We've been over this a hundred times, Daniel. We're doing this"—He waved his hand at me—"for all of us. I'd like her to come, too."

Gideon's gaze was steady and I had to look away.

"Sure," Daniel said. He nodded, then shrugged. "If we survive, this is for all Terminals."

"So what's going on?" I asked. My skin burned in the closed-in room. "Why are you watching TV in here?"

"First, Shiloh, this isn't a TV. It's a computer. A way for us to store information and find out about the real world," Daniel said.

Abigail cleared her throat. "We've found some things out, Shiloh. About the Terminals here at school and other places, too. Around the country, around the world. Some of the hospitals are like our place. Others have horrible conditions for Terminals."

Gideon waited. Daniel peered at her when she spoke.

Listen but don't believe. "Go on."

She waited then said, "We're being used. All of us here. We're being used in awful ways."

For a split second my brain stopped. Everyone breathed the good air for themselves.

We're not taking both lungs. Just one.

I don't want to do this.

It's here for you.

"That is crazy," I said. My lips had turned to butter. "It's preposterous."

I was hit with a memory, from how long ago, I wasn't sure.

"It's preposterous," Principal Harrison said. The Dining Hall was full of Terminals and Teachers. Along the edges, like they held up the walls, were the Whole who worked here, too.

A break-in. Someone—a Whole male—grabbed a young female Terminal.

"Do not begin to let it in your Terminal minds that we do anything illegal here," the principal said in the microphone. "Haven Hospital and Halls is above reproach. We do more than other facilities in providing care."

Now, Gideon spoke. "Daniel and I've known for a while. We stopped taking our Tonic long ago. And we've thought of a plan. One to get us out of here and get help for the rest of the Terminals."

"What plan? This sounds like a lie." As soon as the words were out of my mouth, I remembered more of that day.

The Whole male hollered, causing a scene. "She's all that's left of my daughter."

"Whatever you heard," Principal Harrison said, and he was yelling, too, "it's all a lie." He helped Security bring the intruder down.

"You don't own her." That was Dr. King.

"We paid for her."

"You both signed contracts." Again, Dr. King.

"Drink the Tonic," Nurse said, and we all did. That meal. That night.

All I wanted was dinner. If they'd just let me eat. The whole school was fuzzy. Flat.

The memory jarred me and I stood with Abigail, Gideon, and Daniel and tried to stop remembering. *It's all a lie.* I had covered my ears that day and now I raised my hands to stop those voices.

"I swallowed Tonic until I threw up," I said.

"What are you talking about?" Daniel asked.

I ignored him though I wanted to respond. "Do you have a way to leave now?"

"Yes," Gideon said.

"And I want you to go." Abigail's face was soft in the light.

I was a part of their secret. They had to trust me.

Or.

Protect this world we live in.

I had choices. I didn't have to do anything.

"What else?" The wall was cool under my fingertips, rough.

They all stood close together, touching. *Touching.* Abigail moved nearer to Gideon. His hand rested on Daniel's shoulder.

Nausea swirled over me. "Quit, Abigail," I said. "You're too close to each other. The plague of 2023 started that way."

"I hate teaching Terminals anything new," Daniel said, and I could hear in his voice that he meant it. "She knows only partial truths."

I gagged.

"Shiloh, all these worries you have? They're from our indoctrination," Abigail said. Her voice was gentle. "The Tonic makes us want to vomit when we have any kind of true affection for someone. Humans are supposed to love each other. We're supposed to touch."

"We're Terminal. Not Whole."

Daniel let out a sigh. "*They've* taught us that. They've told us to think that way."

Gideon, whose face seemed pale in the light of the computer, said, "The Tonic is for sleeping and dreams. It takes away our natural affection and makes us obedient. Put that with the music that's always played, the Pledge, what we're told in classes, the low hum of voices in Isolation. What we read, what we study . . . it all works to control us." He looked down, then back to me. "And we *are* human. We're taught otherwise."

"I came with you tonight and I keep drinking the Tonic." Gideon didn't need to know that I had come to warn them to be obedient.

"You're different, Shiloh," Abigail said. "You and I have always gone creeping around at night. You and I have always had a hard time sleeping. We've looked over the wall."

"And it's *more* than obedience," Daniel said. "Haven Hospital and Halls does more than train us."

"Show her," Gideon said.

"Show me what?"

Daniel moved the screen so I could see better. He pulled a typewriter-like keyboard out of a drawer and pressed a few buttons. "The computer will show you, Shiloh," he said.

11

The Haven Hospital & Halls logo, the one on the front of the administration building, was the first picture I saw. Daniel bent closer to the keyboard as all the colors of a rainbow swung around on the screen. A key here. Tap there. "Code," he said, mumbling. He typed something.

Abigail stepped closer, reaching to touch me, but I didn't let her and she pulled back. "Watch a little of this, Shiloh. I couldn't leave if you didn't go with me. I need you to understand."

Why did she keep saying *go*? Where were we supposed to go *to*?

"Watch the commercial on the computer screen, then decide," she said. Her voice was a whisper. "It's sort of like Terminal TV. We have commercials out there, advertising the Hospital and stuff. The real world has commercials, too. Some are for us. Some are against. This computer allows us to access all that information."

"Give me room," I said, "I need some room. I need oxygen. We're too packed in here." Abigail and Gideon shuffled away. I made sure to not touch anyone. The air was hot.

Daniel pressed a few more keys. "This machine is obsolete," he said. "Runs waaay slow. But we've managed to pick up the Iservnet down here. In the admin building there are ones that fly."

"Fly?"

"You know. There are computers that give you the info you need in a millisecond. Press a button, everything is there at your fingertips."

"They use them here?" I asked. "I thought the rays caused cancer?"

"It's a fallacy," Daniel said. "They're lying. It's *all* a lie."

"Haven Hospital and Halls is above reproach." My words came out weak.

"They tell us to say that. We have to think it. They *make* us." Daniel's voice was just as strong.

"Wait. Both of you," Gideon said.

"All right." I nodded and my neck made a slight cracking noise. Already I was breaking apart. *Stay calm.* "So what's at your fingertips?"

"Information. About us," Abigail said. "Terminals in the world."

"Or anything else, for that matter," Gideon said. "The weather. The economy. World powers. Even Dr. King. Anything outside this place. Everything about this place, too."

The screen swirled in colors, and music began. Then came the words, SHOP SO YOU DON'T DROP.

A female, dressed in a red to-the-floor gown, stood at a microphone. Throngs of people cheered for her as she accepted an award, and a sash that read MS. WORLD BEAUTY was placed over her head so it hung from shoulder to hip. The shot moved back, and there was Ms. World Beauty, full screen. Her face was huge. Shiny lips (Why?). Golden hair done up in curls. She looked familiar.

"After my accident, I wondered if I would ever pageant again. Pageanting was my world." There was a shot of an airplane burning. "No one survived this flight but me. I was burned. Disfigured." There was a picture of her in a hospital bed, no hair, no real face. Even her eyes were gone.

"Because I planned ahead, I can live my life still. My Replicant, my Duplicate, made this possible for me. And a Replicant will do this for you, too."

Daniel paused the computer. "Do you recognize her?"

I touched my neck.

"Do you know her?"

"How could I know her?" The air felt like fire. No. That female had been consumed by fire.

"You can't remember?" Gideon said.

"What?"

"Think about it, Shiloh," Gideon said, his voice just louder than the whir of the computer. "Who does she look like?"

The woman on the screen. Her smooth blond hair. Blue eyes. Tiny nose. "She reminds me of Claudia."

Claudia, who had been called out four times, the final time in March of last year, and had never come back. It felt like a hand clutched my windpipe.

Daniel nodded. "You're so smart." He adjusted the sound on the computer.

"By supporting the rights of ourselves we can live, beautifully, for a long, long time," the woman said. Her face faded. A small box popped up on the screen. REPLAY? or CLOSE? it asked.

"Show her your clip," Abigail said.

"No," Daniel said.

"She needs to understand," Gideon said.

Daniel hesitated, then pressed a few buttons. Again, the screen swirled in colors, and a different music began.

"Benefitting the World, One Human Being at a Time," a voice said.

An older male spoke. He looked so like Daniel in the face that I would have thought it *was* him.

"When your body turns against you"—the screen flashed to the male in a hospital bed—"the first thought is suicide. My legs were my life."

A male ran down a grassy field, others chasing after him, their helmets reflecting bright lights. A huge crowd was on its feet.

"Football," Abigail said, and I nodded.

"Then you hear, 'You have *Vibrio vulnificus,* a virulent strain of bacteria,' and the world suddenly looks different." The scene changed with the words, and the male, asleep on a table covered in sheets, had a mask over his face. It was obvious that the surgeons were amputating his legs.

A mask.

I shivered. I'd fought a mask just like that.

"Lucky for me, I invested in myself. My Replicant was there for me. And no matter what tragedy occurs, I'm ready for it." The male walked across a field, all alone this time, tossing a football into the air as he went.

Again the box appeared on the screen. REPLAY? or CLOSE?

"Okay, wait a minute," I said. The words piled into my brain, ramming into each other, trying to make sense. "Claudia was the Replicant for—" I stopped talking. My mouth went dry. It felt like the mask was back, covering my own mouth and nose again, pouring that horrid smell into my lungs—my lung.

Daniel took off his glasses, and his eyes grew huge. "You said she was brilliant. A genius. Photographic memory and such. You said she'd figure it out if we showed her clues."

"Figure it out?" I didn't want to think. Didn't want to feel. Didn't want to remember.

"Listen to this, Shiloh." Gideon played a bit of the news report. Dr. King's face appeared. "We can do anything. Face transplants, limb restoration, increased libido, even give life to those you've lost. *If you're prepared."*

Face transplants, limb restoration, increased libido, even give life to those you've lost.

Rocks replaced my insides. My cheeks cooled.

"You know," Gideon said.

"She can't help us," Daniel said. "And now we've shown her."

"I'm not leaving her behind, Daniel. I'm not," Abigail said.

"Think!" Gideon's voice.

Genetic copies.

I did not want to think.

Replicants. Duplicates.

"I'm going back to my room." I would break in half in this closet. "I'm not coming here again."

I turned, tripping on Daniel's wheelchair, but I caught myself.

Gideon grabbed my arm and squeezed. Sick. I bent a little but refused to let him see what he knew he was doing. He made me face him.

"You know, don't you?" he asked. His breath was hotter than the room. "You know. Say it."

I tried to jerk free. "Let go." My teeth clenched so hard, I thought I might lose a molar. "You know the rules. No contact between Terminals, especially between males and females."

"Right," said Daniel, watching Gideon and me, "because if we loved each other, if we cared about one another, we might fight back." He pushed away from the computer and let out a tired sigh. "I'm going to bed."

"Tell me what you're thinking," Gideon said. He hadn't let go of my arm.

I twisted. My stomach tried to leap from my mouth. But I couldn't give voice to my thoughts. It was too awful. Too *terminal*. His grip tightened.

"You're hurting me, Gideon." I tried to wrench free again. His fingers burned into my arm, all the way to the bone.

"Tell me what you know."

"Stop!" Abigail said. There was no smile. "She doesn't understand. There's no way she can see her connection to all this."

"Oh, she knows," Daniel said. "She just refuses to get it." He opened the door and wheeled away, letting the door close with a click behind him.

"Gideon," Abigail said, and she pulled his hand free of my arm. "Remember how you felt."

"It's us," I said, my voice slipping from between my teeth. *"We're* the body parts for everyone else. Okay? I do get it. It's *us.*"

Gideon released my arm. His hand dropped to his side.

Now I held this secret.

And I didn't want it.

Abigail's shoulders slumped. Her face was pale.

"Yes," she said.

I leaned right into Gideon's face. So close, I felt sick.

"I . . . don't . . . want . . . to . . . know . . . any . . . more."

"You have to," Abigail said. "Or you won't have the courage to run."

"I don't care."

"We need you to get your memory, Shiloh." Gideon sounded exhausted. Like he'd spent a week in Isolation. I should think so, given his defiance.

Abigail said, "I can't leave you here."

As I watched her, just like that, she sprung a leak, and her eyes watered. It was as if they both were broken.

"You're malfunctioning." I felt shaky from the close proximity, because of my own words, because of what I'd seen.

Because of what I knew.

I wanted this all gone! And I never wanted to think of it again. *Take the Tonic. Sleep. No dreams.*

"I'm just crying." She wiped at her face, at the water that reflected the dim light from the computer screen.

"It's one of the things you'll do when you don't drink the Tonic. The medicine keeps us from showing any real emotion." Gideon's words seemed a recitation.

This world of mine, this awful world of mine, seemed to grow darker. "Okay. Okay."

But Abigail didn't seem to be able to stop. She slipped down the wall, till she sat on the floor, dipped her head to her knees. Her shoulders shook.

"Claudia was the Duplicate for Amy Steed," Gideon said. "That pageant queen."

My brain seemed raw.

"And you saw where Daniel's legs went."

"We give our bodies to other people." Had I said those words out loud?

"*They* give our bodies to other people," Gideon said. "*You've* seen the results." He held up his hands like the secret rested there.

"See us, Shiloh," Abigail said. She spoke with her head down. "I mean, *really* see us. Not one of us is whole."

The proof was all around me. Here in the room. And on the computer. In all my classes. The whole of Haven Hospital & Halls.

I sat next to Abigail on the floor.

"There are other ads," Gideon said. "Some of the people we don't recognize. But there are schools like ours all over the country. Haven Hospital & Halls plus lots of others that aren't affiliated with Dr. King."

"This is why we're leaving," Abigail said. "We're going for help."

"What makes you think there's help out there?" I asked. "We're a trade item. We're better than money." I knew the truth as soon as I spoke.

"Shiloh, do you remember when we peeked over the wall?"

I nodded.

"What did you see?"

I shrugged. "Land. The water. The chain-link fence."

"Past that," Abigail said. "Way out there."

"Cars with flashing lights." It had been so warm that day. So nice to be out. "People carrying signs."

"Protestors," Gideon said, "in our defense."

"No," I said, shaking my head. "Protestors want us dead. The Whole don't think Terminals should live. Dr. King—"

"I know. *He* told us so. Or Principal Harrison. Our Teachers. They *tell* us." Gideon bent over the computer. He tapped a few keys, and another ad came on. This time it was a male. He said, "When I lost my Bryan to cancer, I thought about a Replicant." The camera pulled back and the male stood with a female. "We'd saved his DNA, we knew what was available. We loved our boy and wanted him with us."

The female nodded. The sun must have been in her eyes because she squinted.

"We did everything we could to save Bryan with the advances available through modern medicine. But we would never take the life of another human being. Not to keep our son alive. It's not my place to choose who lives and dies. Our boy had a good life. And we want Replicants to have good lives, too."

Gideon paused the commercial.

"There are people out there fighting for us," he said. "And you've seen them. We're not alone."

12

The floor was cold. My hands had gone numb. My brain felt like it might burst open.

"There's more," Abigail said.

Gideon shook his head.

Maybe I couldn't take anything else. Maybe I should never hear another thing. "What?"

"Not yet."

"I will," she said, "if you don't."

"Tell me."

"Do you remember, Shiloh, when that male broke into the facility?" Gideon clasped his hands together in his lap. "He came for the Terminal and tried to take her away?"

I nodded. "That was years ago, but I recall the event. Why?"

Neither of them spoke, then Abigail said, "It was only a few weeks ago, Shiloh."

I rubbed my forehead. "That was when we were younger. All of us were third years. Or fourth at the most."

"The event happened at the beginning of this year," Gideon said. "And the male came for you."

I pushed myself up. "No," I said, drawing the word out. "That's not possible. I would retain that information."

"I was there," Gideon said. "A friend had already convinced me not to use the Tonic, so I remember."

"You're confused." I tried to make the words more than a whisper.

"I'm not. I saw it. You tried to get away. The male grabbed you, pulled you out of the Dining Hall. You fought him. Security came from everywhere. Dr. King grabbed you by the arm and tried to pull you away."

Abigail's eyes were wide and filling with water again.

"The male said you were part of him, Shiloh," Gideon said. "That he was your father and you were all he had left of his daughter, Victoria."

"That can't be. My recollection is of the incident happening a long time ago. To someone else."

"I promise, Shiloh. It was you."

"They take our memories," Abigail said, standing up, too. "And they change them."

"For some of us, like you, it takes more to get rid of the stores of information."

We can get rid of the dreams.

I felt numb all over.

Nurse, telling me to take more and more and more Tonic. Throwing up so much red.

"They are the reason you have to come with us," Abigail said. "Not just that I need you to be with us. Not just your memory."

"Who?" My eyes had dried out. Maybe I would never blink again.

"Your family," Gideon said.

I wanted to say *I have no idea what you're talking about,* but I was too stunned.

Gideon tapped away at the computer. The screen changed. Now there was a female, holding a microphone and standing near the wall.

"That's here," I said. "That's right here." I paused. "How did you get this? It's . . ."

"Contraband," Abigail said, watching the screen. "All of this is."

Gideon edged the sound up.

". . . protests for the life inside the building. But Dr. Franklin King, director of these institutions and hospitals, defends the Haven Hospital and Halls."

Dr. King wore a suit, one that reminded me of what he wore

94

when Visitors stopped by. His hair was slicked back. He smiled and his teeth looked so white. I felt light-headed, weak-kneed. I needed to obey. Instead, I listened, locking my knees.

"The Genetic Copies we house at our hospitals around the world are well cared for. We feed them the best food, teach them of the world, and make sure every need is met."

"Genetic copies," I said.

"You've seen the footage of our hospitals. You know our Copies are fed and clothed and given an education."

Pictures of filthy rooms and dirty unkempt people, many missing body parts and looking infected, popped up.

Dr. King's voice continued. "This place was shut down when it was too late."

Another picture of three starved Terminals stacked next to a wall, one on top of the other.

"But we offer Copies the best of everything, including their dignity."

There was a close-up of the face of a dead Terminal, lips dried out, eyes bugging. Something wormy moved over the skin.

No one in our little room said anything.

"The good we accomplish far outweighs the negative view some more conservative"—Dr. King hesitated. . . . A smile crept to his lips—"thinkers might have. Our facilities are the finest. The Copies live a life of luxury. They are not herded together like cattle or, worse, like poultry, but live respectful lives."

There was footage then of Haven Hospital & Halls. I recognized the Dining Hall. Terminals gathered to eat. This was old. Abigail was just back from surgery. She looked like she was in pain, being fed by Mr. Oliver, a teacher who left some time ago. All the Terminals' heads were down while they ate. No one looked up. There was no sound but the clinking of silverware.

The camera turned back to the reporter.

"And there are plenty of conservative thinkers fighting against Dr. King and his claims."

"Watch this part, Shiloh," Gideon said. "This is important."

A new female voice. "When you allow your DNA to be duplicated, when someone is grown for you, you, the investor, lose all your rights and privileges to the creator of your Duplicate." The female hesitated. "These are children. There are babies, too, being farmed, being grown in these places."

A woman with dark brown eyes looked out at us. My stomach dropped. I knew her. Had seen her somewhere before. She sat next to a man. A memory knocked at my brain.

"Children. Humans. Not just Duplicates—not just Genetic Copies." Behind her, people marched, chanting and carrying signs that said WE ALL HAVE A RIGHT TO LIFE. And WE *USE* REPLICANTS. And A HEART IS A HEART. The camera steadied again on the woman's face.

"Fair treatment is all I ask for those who cannot defend themselves," she said. "And that we be allowed to own what we have paid for. Our country has protections for the rights of the old and the young, the weak and those who can't care for themselves. Now *we* want *our* rights back."

The screen froze. Gideon clicked the computer off. No one spoke for a long while. Gideon swung around in the chair. "When we found this information"—he waved his hand back behind him—"I recognized that male from when he came to get you."

Abigail spoke. "I knew you needed to be a part of this. Because *they* want you."

"You're a link to the outside. And you're our link, too."

"If we get out, Shiloh," Abigail said, "you can go to them. We can help ourselves, and others, too. We need to find those who are out there for each of us. Then we'll be free. We can live like normal people. Not like wares someone buys and, in the process, destroys."

Gideon cleared his throat. "You have a family, Shiloh."

My lips had dried out. My tongue felt useless. "But I'm not theirs. She said she has no right to me. That means Haven Hospital and Halls owns me."

"That's true of all of us," Abigail said.

"Even if my Recipient is gone," I said, "Haven Hospital and Halls will still sell me to others I might match up with."

"You're right," Gideon said. "You don't have to be an exact DNA match to give your parts. Doctors have used that method of saving others for generations."

I looked at my hands. The nails were just the right length. The same as all other Terminals who still had their arms and hands. I was missing a lung. Part of me went to someone else. I was a Terminal, yes. A Copy. A Replicant. And like what had happened with Claudia, I would be used as much as I was needed. "All of us will die like Claudia," I said.

"Unless we stop it," Gideon said.

I recalled parts of the moment when the doors had swung open and that male had come to the Dining Hall.

He'd grabbed that Terminal.

It was you!

Tried to carry her away.

Not her! You!

She'd fought him.

I *had fought him.*

And given away my freedom.

"We're not alone," Abigail said. "Shiloh, we have each other. And the Whole out there, the ones you saw protesting, if we get away. You have people waiting."

I couldn't even nod.

"This's enough for one night," Gideon said. "Go back to your rooms. Don't make lengthy eye contact with each other tomorrow. Don't talk to anyone you shouldn't. And no one speaks of this meeting. Anyone who talks will have to be disposed of."

I blinked, trying to soothe my dry eyes.

"We have to defend ourselves and our Cause," he said.

"I understand." My voice didn't sound like me at all. Maybe I now used the voice of the person who had my lung.

Abigail and I walked back in darkness, sticking to the blackest shadows, out of the way so no one would see us.

"Why didn't you tell me sooner?" I asked.

Abigail touched my elbow with a fingertip. "I didn't know how. And I haven't known that long. It's been over a month since I walked in on Daniel and Gideon."

There was no sound here in the basement except the pad of our feet on the stone floor.

"We always explore together," I said. "It's like you fooled me."

"No, Shiloh, it wasn't that at all." Abigail stopped.

I waited, arms folded.

"I couldn't sleep. I tried to wake you and you wouldn't budge. You'd been taking the Tonic a lot, for dreams and maybe so you would forget about the male coming for you. You wouldn't wake up. So, I left on my own."

I rested against the wall. I felt too tired to go on.

"That night I saw Daniel going down the hallway and I followed. At first, I thought maybe he was a spirit or something."

I understood that.

"So I followed him, but I didn't bother them. You and I sneak around. I figured it was the same thing."

I waited.

"I got up again. I had a vague memory of the wheelchair and I wanted to see if I could find Daniel on my own."

"Okay."

"You were sound asleep that night, too. In fact, you'd not gotten out of bed for days, you slept like you were . . ." She paused.

I knew. "Like I was dead."

Abigail let out a long sigh. "I knew you were alive. I put my finger under your nose to see if you were breathing." Her hand went to her stomach like the remembering caused her discomfort.

"That time I saw Gideon. He came in from outside and he had snow on his jacket. He told me about the resistance, about the Cause, and here I am." She raised her palm up. "Isaac had just been taken away."

"But that happened last week."

She shook her head. "The Tonic messes up time. Slows it down. Speeds it up."

We started again toward our room. My insides trembled, like my muscles might fall from the bone.

"Daniel and Gideon told me everything, including the break-in by the male."

We were in the hall outside our room. Over the fireplace I could see the clock and the time. It was almost two in the morning. We'd only been gone two hours? How could that be? It felt like weeks had passed since I'd dreamed of ripping off Gideon's arm.

"And then," Abigail said, "Isaac didn't come back."

We hurried to our beds, past Mary and Elizabeth, who both slept without moving.

I stepped out of my clothes and folded them, placing the pants in the bottom drawer and the T-shirt in with the other old work clothing. I pulled pajamas out from under my pillow and slipped them on.

Then I climbed into bed, turned over—back to the window—and closed my eyes.

From across the room came Abigail's voice. "They let me join, Shiloh, because I know you. You are our hope."

I didn't answer.

Do you have your suitcase?

It's there. By the dresser.

You won't be gone long.

I don't want her to come.

She's part of the plan. To see what will happen.

No.

Get your things, please.

I nod. Start the walk. It's so far. The corridor is dark as a hole. Cold as the snow. There are voices. And a screen with blue lights.

Then I am on the bed. Something cries out. Once more.

The voice echoes. Comes into my mind over and over.

We'll get rid of the Disease. Send this heart where it belongs. Stop them from taking over the world. Put things back to normal.

Brightness stabs at my eyes. It's in the back of my head, sharp. The light shines on faces. One I don't recognize.

No! she says.

I've changed my mind, she says. I don't care what I've signed.

There's the knife, slicing down my breastbone, opening me up, like chicken in the kitchen.

I'm the only one who survived this crash.

Hands reach, pull out the blackness that fills me. Tug it away. It aches, tears. I feel the tendons separating from the bone. The blackness turns to blood.

Look at my legs.

They have my heart. Steam rises. I smell something awful.

I'm in the hall.

No heart, one lung, Daniel in his wheelchair. Abigail motions for me to follow her. There's Gideon.

We'll take more than your heart, he says, smiling.

They sew me up.

But the bleeding will not stop.

From the corner of the room, I see her.

The female who shakes her head, and she leaves.

HAVEN
HOSPITAL & HALLS
Where You Matter

Established 2020

Note to all Staff

Please be aware and report all murmurings and unusual behavior as we discussed in Faculty Meetings: facial changes, thoughtful discussion, being too alert.

Report these and any other worries to school officials.

We must keep all Terminals, and you, safe from the outside world.

13

"Abigail?" I said into the dark room. "Abigail?"

There was no answer. So she slept fine if she stayed up late enough, even without the Tonic.

The female in the commercial. Her voice in my dreams. She'd had me made for her, right? For her daughter?

I thought of Claudia. All that blond hair. Her blue eyes. Skin clear as porcelain. Used-up pageant girl.

If I had been a little older, I would have been in Claudia's class. I might have shared a room with her. I might have known her better.

All these Terminals. All of us waiting to be harvested. Like the greenhouse vegetables here. Waiting to be used. To save someone else's life by giving our own.

It's not true.

But I had seen it myself.

I pulled the covers over my head.

No more dreams. I didn't want to feel uneasy. Didn't want to be here anymore.

But what could I do? I remembered Abigail crying. Not just the sounds a Terminal makes when they're hurt, but that water on her face.

Fight.

I'd rather fight.

I'd rather get away.

Save the Terminals, like Gideon said. Like Abigail and Daniel said.

Save myself.

Have a bit of the promise.

There were no promises here except that our lives would end.

I rolled over. It was still dark outside.

Right before I fell asleep, I remembered Gideon saying he wanted me to go with them, too.

I tried to make my face smile at the memory, but it just wouldn't.

It wasn't so easy to not drink the Tonic. Even though no one looked to see if we did. They trusted we would. And we did. I mean, we always had. *I* always had. Why check on something that is so secure already?

We were, all of us, creatures of habit.

Trained.

Still I felt I *must* drink that Tonic. Go to bed at night. Down the Tonic. Get up in the morning, drink the Tonic. Take in a breath, let it out. Stand when you are called from lunch. Walk down the hall with the others. Sleep when Brahms begins. Awake with Mozart. Give your arm. Give your lung. Give something that might keep *you* alive.

The next morning, I reached for that little cup sitting on my nightstand. Not even sitting up all the way, I readied to swallow the drink. My body told me to. My hand reached out on its own.

Wait!

I swung my legs over the side of the bed. Everyone got ready. Morning called. Time to begin the day.

I will be free. Will fight to be free.

My hand shook as I set the cup aside. Abigail raised her cup to me then turned her back. When she looked at me again, I saw a bit of the red juice on her lips, the color of Amy Steed's dress.

Fine—I could do it, too. I tossed the drink in my mouth, then hurried to the bathroom. The insides of my cheeks stung.

Go, go, go.

I pushed through into the bathroom, walked into a stall, locked the door behind me, and spit everything in the toilet, washing the bright red liquid away with a flush.

A few sips of that drink. A couple of ounces? Who would think it could control me?

When I stood, my head banged. A headache. A splitter of a headache. Even my ears hurt.

"You okay, Shiloh?" Abigail. I saw her feet on the tiles outside where I crouched.

"My head hurts," I said. I opened the door, went to the sink, splashed water on my face. The overhead light stabbed at my eyes. The pain under my skull was so intense, it pounded through my skin.

"Listen," Abigail said as Elizabeth hurried in to dress. Our roommate nodded to our reflections in the mirror and we nodded back. Elizabeth went into the stall I had been in.

"Oh, this is bad," Elizabeth said. "Someone didn't flush and I don't know what's in the toilet."

She came out of the stall, her clothes folded in her arms. The skin on her face was red and puckered, cut close to the bone.

Abigail flushed the toilet again. "I've seen that happen," she said to Elizabeth. "The water is red. A couple of tries and it goes away. Don't give it another thought. I took care of it."

"I won't," Elizabeth said.

Okay, so down the toilet didn't work. Then where? My head throbbed. I wet a washcloth in cool water and buried my face in it. I heard Elizabeth go into a different stall.

"The pain starts right away, if you're a few hours late taking the Tonic," Abigail said in a hushed tone, turning the faucet on full blast. Sounds stabbed at my ears. "Whatever you do, act normal. This won't last long but you have to be sure you don't let anyone know. Terminals don't notice. The staff might. You complain of anything, they'll give you a double dose and force you to take it. There's supposed to be a cure, but we haven't found it yet."

I nodded.

"You're addicted and you're coming off the stuff, whatever it is. Remember, they control you. I promise it doesn't last long."

I'd heard of addictions. Terminals left Haven Hospital & Halls because they needed help from the outside to make them better—relieve them of the addictions they somehow got here. When they returned, those Terminals looked so spent, so worn out, I couldn't even begin to wonder what it was that had been done to them.

"Okay," I said.

In class, it felt like someone had hit me in the back of the head with a tree trunk. I went through the motions almost unable to see, my head hurt so.

Ms. Iverson quieted us clapping—just as she does every day—and the sound was like someone banging on a pot lid inside my skull. I felt the vibrations in my cheeks.

"Are you okay, Shiloh?" she asked. She had opened a book, waiting for the rest of us to follow her. Daniel sort of looked over at me. Abigail didn't even make a sound. "Are you ill?"

"Oh, I'm fine, Ms. Iverson," I said. A lie popped into my head. "I stayed up too late reading for class." I held the book *Lord of the Flies* aloft. "I know I shouldn't have, but now I'm tired."

I blinked. I had never, *never* lied before because I had to. My nerves jangled.

"No more late nights, Shiloh," Ms. Iverson said. "They're not good for you." She sat on her desk. "Still, I'm glad you like this bit of nonfiction. We can learn a lot about sacrifice and good-doing from the death of Piggy."

"Yes, ma'am."

In his seat in front of me, Gideon shifted. He seemed to have not heard a thing I said. Could anyone hear the banging in my head? How had this happened to the three of them and I not noticed?

"Listen," Abigail said at lunch. My face felt fat with the pain. Swollen. "You keep right on pretending you are who you *were*. Watch what everyone else does and you do it. A few more days and we're out of here."

Abigail stood beside me, encouraging me to put more and more and more food on the plate.

"Keep going," Abigail said. "You have to keep up with your previous intake of nutrition. The staff notices these kinds of things. It's their job." She nodded at me. "And anyway, the more in your system, the faster the Tonic clears out."

I picked up my fork, seeing it tremble in my hand. It took a great effort to eat. My plate was full. Piled high. How did I consume so much before?

And then those side doors opened.

Even with my headache, I jerked my head up. The movement caused pain to shoot down my shoulders and into my palms. I dropped the fork and it spun a couple of times before it fell to the floor. When I leaned over, my skull threatened to explode off the top of my body.

Those doors. So tall. So slow. It was a torture to watch. There was that bit of a squeak, and the whole room went quiet.

I couldn't move. No one moved.

Not any of us.

We waited.

Count! the voice in my head said. *Protect yourself. Protect Abigail. And Gideon. And Daniel and the rest of the Terminals. Count!*

Ms. Iverson didn't look up from her plate. Mr. MacGee settled his napkin in his lap.

"Hello, Terminals," Dr. King said. His voice boomed in my ears, turned my brain to jelly. A boiling emotion came up inside me, one that had never before filled me about Dr. King.

He was the reason we were all here. *He* was responsible. I had to look away or I might scream.

He waved, stepping through the sun that fell to the floor in a golden puddle. The sun seemed a lie, too.

Principal Harrison took huge steps, following behind Dr. King, like he needed to catch up. He fingered his ponytail. To the stage they went. Up the stairs while someone ran for the mic.

Dr. King waved again and Principal Harrison held out his hands. There wasn't a sound in the room.

Abigail reached for me, and I let her touch me. My stomach didn't swirl as much, but it felt like a band played in my forehead using my eyeballs as the cymbals.

One . . .

two . . .

three . . .

four . . .

What was wrong with me? I would lose us all if I didn't speed up.

five . . .

six . . .

seven . . .

"Don't worry," Abigail said. Her face was pale. "Don't worry."

I couldn't let her voice in my head. It must be the headache's fault. Because I wasn't taking the Tonic.

You should take it!

No! Count!

ten . . .

eleven . . .

twelve . . .

Just make it to fifty before they say the name. You don't have to go to a hundred. Get to fifty.

"Whatever you do, Shiloh, whoever it is, don't make a sound."

Focusing on Abigail's face was difficult, but I nodded at her words.

sixteen . . .

seventeen . . .

eighteen . . .

nineteen . . .

"We have reports back now for . . ."

Hopelessness crashed through me. I wouldn't make the countdown. I wouldn't even get as far as usual and maybe, because of me, someone I knew . . .

No one made a sound.

twenty . . .

". . . for Elizabeth."

I gasped. Elizabeth?

Our Elizabeth?

She startled. Dropped her spoon, still holding tomato basil soup, and it pinged against the table, splashing on her shirt. Her face went red and I saw that her black hair had been pulled back in a perfect braid. There were tiny pink ribbons at the bottom and top of her hair.

"I don't want to go," Elizabeth said to me and Abigail. "I want to stay here. I don't want to go."

"Of course you do," Principal Harrison said. How had he heard her? "There's something wrong and we must take care of it. Ms. Iverson, please help Elizabeth get her prepared bag."

Ms. Iverson hesitated, then nodded once. She pushed back her chair. "It'll be okay," Ms. Iverson said. "Elizabeth, finish your lunch. I'll go get your things."

Abigail didn't look at me. The whole Dining Hall seemed to grow smaller, tighter.

"Don't make eye contact with her." The words floated over to me. Had Dr. King heard that? Abigail ate a bit of wilted spinach. Her hands shook.

A lie! A lie! Aliealiealiealiealie . . . My mind didn't want to stop. Pain thumped with the words. Aliealiealie.

Elizabeth turned to her food. She ate in slow motion. Now only two splotches of rose colored her cheekbones.

"Get back to lunch," Dr. King said. "Eat up." Then he looked at me as though he could see my missing parts.

I swallowed. Would I break eye contact if I drank my morning Tonic. Maybe I wouldn't? I forced myself to eat. To not look back up. I devoured the lean lamb and the new lettuce (like some I had helped plant), along with the tiny grilled eggplant that was not even three inches long yet.

"Whatever you do, Shiloh . . ." Abigail spoke through the food in her mouth. She ate large bites. Her eyes were squinty. "—remember to be like everyone else. Don't draw attention to yourself.

Be like them." She gestured with her chin at the rest of the Terminals.

They all ate. Some slower than others. Maybe Elizabeth's being chosen had unsettled them. Or relieved them? But the rest of the lunchroom of Terminals ate with little talking. They were all intent on getting every last bit cleaned off their plates.

Like I had been.

"I don't want to go," Elizabeth said. Her plate was empty.

Ms. Iverson came up behind Elizabeth. I hadn't seen her reenter the Dining Hall. "Ready, Elizabeth?"

Elizabeth shook her head no, but she stood, back straight. Her braid went all the way to the pale blue belt at her hips.

I wanted to say good-bye, wanted to say anything, but I ate the eggplant that tasted almost too bitter to swallow.

14

The day went on forever. I was haunted by Dr. King's stare, by Elizabeth's straight back, by her not wanting to go. All day a lump the size of a fist sat in my throat, making it difficult to swallow.

And the pain. I couldn't get away from it. No matter how I tried, it was there. In every part of my body, places I hadn't even known I had before. All of it hurt.

That night, when it was time to get ready for bed, I walked in slow motion to the shower. Cupping the Tonic in both hands, I tried to keep the medicine steady and not spill it. Never had I wanted to drink the nighttime Tonic more.

Even though I'd showered this morning, I had to again. Sweat seemed to pour off me. My shirt was damp. I'd thrown up three times. Even the soles of my feet hurt.

In the shower, I knelt. My body *wanted* to give up. I was so compelled to drink that my hands trembled as cool water splashed around me.

"Do it," I said. "Do it." Water ran in my mouth as I whispered. My eyes felt swollen.

At last, I tipped the drink out of the cup and watched it swirl away, thinning to pink as it went.

The water pounded on my chest. My scalp was so sensitive, I didn't think I could stand even a drop to hit my head.

"You'll be better soon." But I wasn't sure. There were too many things I suffered from to just "get better."

Like that, I felt the scream from my dreams tearing up from inside, from below my stomach. I bit my lip to stop the sound. I bit till a chunk of flesh came off and blood seeped into my mouth. I spit over and over, watching the red wash away like the Tonic had.

I kept seeing Elizabeth's ribboned braid. Hearing her voice, that she didn't want to go. Seeing her stand so tall.

The lump in my throat grew bigger.

I remembered them all, the Terminals who had left, one by one. Sometimes straight-backed like Isaac had gone. Others not wanting to leave, like Elizabeth.

All had been afraid.

I stayed on the tile until my knees ached. When I knew I couldn't wait any longer, I got up. Gentle as I could, I washed my hair, almost not touching my head. The soapy water ran over my body, over my scar.

All of them being called out. James and Madeleine and Chloe. Bartholomew and Marte and then three males, all in a row—Seth,

Jacob, and Peter. There was Damaris and Leah and me and Abigail. Mark, Edna, Lydia, Ruth, Miriam. Claudia. Isaac. Elizabeth.

Sometimes they came back.

Sometimes . . .

Worry coursed through me.

I wanted to run, escape, try to get away, even with this massive headache.

Their eyes. Their faces.

I had been terrified.

Don't think of that.

Think obedience.

The voice was dimmer. Not so strong.

One step at a time. Just one at a time. I faced the water, let it hit my cheekbones. I could do this.

Rinse.

Get out of the shower.

Dry off.

No running.

Get dressed for bed.

Make it through the next day.

Abigail and Gideon and Daniel were right. We had to fight. Had to free those who couldn't free themselves. We might be able to stop innocent Terminals from dying.

If I had the courage.

Even if I had this headache the rest of my life.

I turned the water to cold, hoping the water would beat the unsteadiness from my body, then tried to follow my own commands.

The room felt empty with Elizabeth gone.

I couldn't swallow at all now.

When the lights went out, I crawled from my bed. The muscles in my neck were so tight, I couldn't relax. No wonder everyone met at night. They couldn't sleep. I went to the window and checked the gazebo. Overhead, the moon was so full, it looked like it might pop. The thought made my stomach turn over.

A warm wind had blown through that morning and all traces of snow had melted. Spring was here. And the promise? Hard to say anything about promise when I felt like this. And with Elizabeth gone.

"Just a few more hours, Shiloh," Abigail said from her bed. "It's a pretty quick detox from whatever they give us. Turns out they can't operate while the drugs are in our system."

"What are you talking about?"

Abigail came to where I stood. She had folded up the flannel of her pajama arm where part of her body was missing and pinned the cloth together. Who taught her to do that?

"When we donate," she said, "if there are any traces of the Tonic in our systems, they can't give the parts to the Recipient. You'll be better by tomorrow afternoon. I promise. That's about how long it took me."

I groaned. Tomorrow afternoon? I looked out the window again. Nothing. No one. I went to bed at last, Elizabeth's braid and those perfectly tied ribbons the last things I remembered.

In the morning, my eyes buzzed. They jittered in my skull.

The pain was so intense, I couldn't open them all the way.

Mary moved around the room. Her bare feet on the carpet sounded amplified.

"What is it, Shiloh?" Mary asked, from where she brushed back her short hair.

I pressed my hands to my forehead, tried to relieve the searing pain. If I could sit up, I'd drink the Tonic. I would. I didn't care what I had thought in the shower last night. This was awful. Horrible!

"Do you need meds?" Abigail asked. She sat on her made bed, legs crossed, book resting in her lap. Everything in the room was underwater blurry.

"No." I'm not sure how I got the word out. "I'm okay."

She was to my side before I could say anything else. I was so confused, I thought she had gone to the Dining Hall already. Her face seemed too large as she bent near. Was this a dream? Why did her face grow and shrink like that?

"It's almost over," she said. And then, she sneaked the Tonic away from my bedside table. If I'd had the energy, I would have fought her for it. "Remember you want to choose."

"I can't do this," I said.

"I'll tell Ms. Iverson if you want me to, Shiloh," Mary said. She stood next to Elizabeth's bed, her hand on the pillow. Then, "I miss Elizabeth."

A jolt ran through me.

"I better"—Mary hesitated—"I better go get some extra Tonic."

Abigail seemed far away and then too close.

"We've got to get you dressed," she said. Her hand was cool on my face. "You have the fever. You'll be better soon. I promise."

One-handed, Abigail helped me faster than I could have dressed myself.

"If you've taken more Tonic, it'll take longer to get it out of your system."

"I haven't." I gagged with the words.

The hardest part was doing my hair. It was so curly, so long and thick, Abigail couldn't pull the brush through with one hand. And my scalp. It felt like my scalp was being ripped away. Like it bled.

"Have I ever told you I love your hair, Shiloh?" Abigail asked.

"No." Bile rose to the back of my throat.

"I have this stick-straight hair. And yours is so full and big." The brush tugged at my tangles. "After I came off the Tonic, I saw how pretty you are." She spoke in tones that reminded me of chocolate. "Remember how you played Nurse in *Romeo and Juliet*?" I couldn't nod. "*This* is the biggest role you'll ever play. As sick as you are, as sick as you get, you have to act normal. Otherwise someone will find us out."

I tried not to think of Elizabeth. Could we save her? Or would we be too late?

All the way down the hallway, slower Terminals around us, Abigail sent me words of encouragement.

"You can do it."

"Just a little longer."

"I swear breakfast will help."

"*We* did it."

"Think about getting out of here."

"Think of Elizabeth."

And always, always, "Act normal."

But what was normal?—I could only remember the pounding in my brain.

The smell of vegan sausages made my mouth water and my stomach heave at the same time.

"Eat," Abigail said.

"Fill your plate, Shiloh," Ms. Iverson said. All around the dining room, the sounds of forks and knives clinking against china were so loud, it felt like a giant ate at my brain.

In the line, my appetite came back. I was starving. Ravenous. I filled my plate with rye waffles and fresh strawberries. When I poured milk from the glass pitcher, I had to use both hands.

At the table I sat across from Abigail, who raised her eyebrows at me.

"We're meeting tonight," she said. "Same time." She ate like she wasn't talking.

I nodded, almost not moving my neck, and pain shot down my back to my heels. The muscles around my spine contracted. This is how I felt after surgery. Cramps everywhere, burning in my skin, pain with every shallow breath. Fire. Ice.

So so sick. I'd forgotten that till right now.

"Okay." Would my face explode on the table? The thought was a bit satisfying. A Replicant with no face. What good would I be to them then?

Was this what the Tonic suppressed? Were these emotions real? If only the pain would go away, maybe I could understand and act as a normal Terminal.

I waded through classes. Each step agonizing. Each breath like fingernails clawing at my lung. Could the other Terminals see me sweating? Or the Teachers? Or Ms. Iverson, who seemed to watch me side-eyed?

Then, just like that, not long after lunch as I walked to Study Hall, I was better.

One minute my head was about to blow up. The next, the pain was gone. I could see. I could hear. My heart wasn't jumping out of my chest. My face still felt tender, and I couldn't turn my head without my neck sending pain everywhere, but the headache, the nausea, the agony in every step were gone.

I could think. And I noticed what Abigail meant by wanting me to act the same as before.

All the Terminals were slow, hesitant. Their faces were tense. Their movements were deliberate. One step at a time. Teachers walked with confidence, heads held high. When they spoke, their mouths didn't sound full of marbles.

But everyone else walked as a group, like geese flying in formation or a school of fish veering off in the same direction.

The difference between the Whole and Terminals was clear. The Tonic had kept shades over my eyes so I couldn't see.

Is that what I had been? All this time? Barely moving?

I stumbled, trying to imagine myself like the rest of the Terminals here. I had been afraid. Worried of the Disease. Of being called out during lunch. Sure.

But I hadn't realized that I had no personality. That's why a smile frightened me, I thought, looking over everyone. Those Terminals' faces showed no emotion. It was like they weren't alive at all.

This is what the outside world, what the Whole, saw in all those commercials.

Blank faces, glazed eyes. No wonder when someone stopped taking the Tonic it was obvious. This is what Visitors saw. Terminals who weren't really alive—so they could be used to death.

I kept pace with everyone.

These Terminals, I realized with a stab of unaccustomed emotion, were my friends.

Someone bumped into me, and I saw her curl forward from the touch.

The hall was quiet, even with the movement of everyone heading off to their respective classes. Shuffling filled the air. Why hadn't I seen this before? I almost stopped to watch. But that wouldn't be normal. Dr. King would know in a minute, the moment I stepped out of line.

15

"I have a secret," Abigail said.

"What?" We were off to a different basement room. The meeting places changed to make it harder to find us. "Terminals don't have secrets."

There was a new voice in my mind. It started as the headache grew less and less. It said things like, *Don't they know everything about us anyway? What can we do about that? They know how we move and think and breathe.* As the pain in my neck and shoulders disappeared, worry replaced it.

Not only was there a new voice, there was a new way of looking at things.

Even in the dark like tonight, lines were more distinct—not smudged as they had been before.

"Tell me your secret," I said.

Abigail paused. She let her face crack open with a smile. "I like someone."

"What do you mean? Of course you like someone. You like everyone. Terminals get along."

"No," Abigail said, her voice hushed and warm. "Different than that." She put her hand to her cheek. Would I make these gestures, too? Would my words come out so mushy?

"I like Daniel." She swallowed with a gulp. "I think he's beautiful."

All around us, the grays of the darkness pushed close. "I've never seen anything beautiful," I said. "What do you mean?"

"You'll see things of beauty from now on, Shiloh. Now that you're getting better."

"Okay." I drew out the word.

"Including males. Especially males."

My stomach dropped a bit. *That's* what she meant? "Terminal males are off-limits. We don't do anything with them more than classroom associations." A bit of the morning's pain stabbed at my shoulders. I stepped back.

"You'll see what I mean," she said.

I would have shaken my head no, but I was afraid the pain might slap at me again. "Maybe." I shrugged even though I knew she couldn't see me in the darkness. "I don't know."

And then, up ahead, I heard voices.

Not Daniel.

Not Gideon.

I stopped. Put my hand out. Abigail clutched at my shirt, pulled me back. We shrank into the shadows. I thought to try and get away but knew that we'd be found if I did that. Fear flashed like light behind my eyes. My head pounded and I worried the detox would happen all over again.

Abigail's face seemed to be made of a million gray and grayer dots. She leaned back into a tiny alcove I hadn't even known was there and disappeared from view. "No matter what happens, don't say anything."

I slid back next to her.

Whispers floated down the hall.

What Terminal was awake now? Who made that much noise? Didn't they know the dangers? How they put us all at risk?

There was the sound of shoes in the hallway. A male's voice. Deep tones. And a female's, too. Soft. Lighter.

They appeared like phantoms, a shade at a time as they drew closer.

Ants ran over and through me. Ms. Iverson.

With Mr. Tremmel.

"This cannot be," Abigail said in my ear. I swatted at her, but missed.

I saw them as one being. They were connected, somehow. Touching. Were they tied together? Mr. Tremmel's arm was around Ms. Iverson's shoulder. And her arm was wrapped around his waist. She threw her head back, covered her mouth with her hand. They stopped a few paces away. In just three steps, I could have been by Ms. Iverson's side.

Abigail gripped my arm. Shook her head. "*Quiet.*" She almost didn't say the words. "*No.*"

Ms. Iverson murmured. Then Mr. Tremmel pulled Ms. Iverson close. He put his mouth to hers, like he would suck her life away.

I gasped and Abigail pulled at my shirt.

Ms. Iverson's arms went up and around Mr. Tremmel's neck. She couldn't even stand on her own, but had to be held up. What was going on? This was dangerous. Deadly.

I should go help her but I closed my eyes. Opened them again to peek at what occurred in the hallway. I couldn't give up the Cause, not even for Ms. Iverson.

Ms. Iverson and Mr. Tremmel stood there, mouths pressing together. Didn't they have any idea what kind of germs they spread?

Mr. Tremmel pulled away from Ms. Iverson and to my complete surprise she did not fall to the ground dead. Instead, she ran her hand down the side of his face, rested her fingertips near his lips.

"We don't have much time," she said. Then they were gone, making way more noise than they should.

I blinked. "He didn't kill her," I said, relieved.

Abigail shook her head. "No." And her voice was solemn. "I've seen a whole documentary on that with Gideon and Daniel. There're several parts to it. It's called *One Life to Live.*"

"They have documentaries on spreading germs?"

"It's called kissing," Abigail said. When she spoke again, she sounded reverent. "I've done that with Daniel."

"What?" I thought I might swallow my tongue. It felt slippery as raw fish.

We walked again and I was shaky, jittery. Abigail looked so pleased. Not a bit the way I felt . . . disgusted at the germ sharing—the possibility of who-knows-what.

"It's not like what they've taught us here," she said. "We should be together."

I didn't answer.

"We should touch. Care."

"How do you know?" My voice was a shallow whisper.

She shrugged, her shoulders almost not lifting. "It's just right. Terminals are meant to be with each other. Like the Whole are. Not only in classrooms. Not separated the way we are."

I took a deep breath. "Are you telling me you put your lips on his?"

"It was fun," Abigail said. "His mouth was so warm. And his lips were soft." She closed her eyes. "And his tongue . . ."

"I don't want to know," I said. "Yuck!"

Abigail raised her eyes at me. "I won't tell you every detail. Some of it's private."

"I think maybe I'll skip this part of being off the Tonic," I said.

Abigail linked her arm with mine. When my stomach swirled, I swallowed away the nausea. "Sure you will," she said.

16

"This is what we're fighting against," Gideon was saying when we came in the room. Daniel's wheelchair was close to the computer. I looked at him, hard. Did *I* want to press my lips on his? I edged around for a better view.

He looked fine. Like anyone else, I suppose. His lips were full. His glasses reflected the computer screen.

"What are you looking at, Shiloh?" Daniel asked.

A tingle of surprise went through me. *Your lips,* I wanted to say but instead said, "Nothing." My cheeks heated up.

"What's wrong?" Abigail asked Gideon. She took my hand and I held on tight. Her touch was warm, soft. I was getting used to this intimacy. The sickness lessened with each caress. I could see this unusual way of communicating—by letting your own skin brush against someone else—could be a comfort. I looked at Daniel again.

Maybe I could see the reasoning for pressing lips together.

He glanced at me like I had done something wrong.

"We found something last night," Gideon said. "New information."

He tapped keys, and the screen changed. Dr. King and the female who wanted me. Her blond curly hair was tamed back in a clasp of some sort.

"It's her," I said.

"Yes," Gideon said. "She's debating Dr. King."

I swallowed. "Why her?"

"She's an advocate for Terminals the world over." When Daniel spoke, his voice was so flat, I almost didn't hear him. He sounded Terminal. "This is about if we're worthy to live."

Gideon turned up the sound.

125

"The question here isn't what others are saying, Ann," Dr. King said.

Ann.

I wanted to see everything about her. Make myself remember what she looked like.

"We can have too many rules in society. These Replicants—or Duplicates, or Copies, whatever you want to call them—they have no souls. These are not people. They are property. They were not made by the union of two people. They were made by me—by *my* abilities." Dr. King held his hands out for her to see, then rested both hands on his chest.

"The argument," Ann said, "is that they *are* human, Dr. King. They deserve the rights any human would because they live and breathe and have feelings and emotions."

Dr. King shifted, leaning closer to Ann, and his face grew larger on the screen. "They have no emotions. You've seen them. You've seen the footage from the schools."

She said nothing.

I thought of what I had seen today. A hallway of Terminals, going to class, heads down, walking in the same fashion, almost taking the same steps together.

That wasn't our fault, I wanted to tell the female. *Ann.* We did what we were programmed to do.

Dr. King's face was earnest. "They are body parts. Just a product. *I* am their god, Ms. Alexander."

Ann looked surprised. "That's an arrogant statement, don't you think?"

"Not when it's the truth." Dr. King appeared confident.

"There's a natural process. We all must die."

"There *was* a natural process. I've all but stopped it. Imagine. You're in a car accident. Your family member is on life support. For all intents and purposes, dead. Before, we took parts from those who had died and gave them to others so *they* could live. The dead were our heroes."

"I know the history of medicine, Dr. King."

Dr. King kept speaking as though she had said nothing. "Now we have the solution to save the lives of those who would have been donors. With today's technologies, with Haven Hospitals and Halls, we can have an exact match for you. We can save your loved ones. And you know about losing someone you love, don't you?"

"I do, Dr. King." A bright light showed on Ann's face. "It is the daughter I lost and her Replicant who are part of my inspiration to stop you. And the rest of the Terminals you lord over."

He paused, opened his mouth, closed it. He looked right out the screen at us and I jumped back.

"He can't see you, Shiloh," Abigail said. "He's not in there."

Just like that, I was sweating. "I know. But it feels like he can see *into* me."

"I aim to put you out of business," Ann said.

Dr. King bowed his head. "I understand loss, too. I lost my own son, my own boy, not that long ago."

Ann's voice was sympathetic. "I know that history, too, Dr. King. He didn't agree with you and your hospital. Your son didn't want a Copy to keep him going, did he?"

"Why would you say that?" Dr. King's voice was broken.

"He and your ex-wife were killed, and you couldn't save either one even though you had the technology."

"That's sad," Abigail said.

"Why is that sad? *His* son made a choice. *He* had the choice," Daniel said. "What do we get?"

"We can save people," Dr. King was saying. "Even if my boy didn't understand and made other choices, there is the technology to keep others living well for a long time. It's my mission for others *because* of my boy."

"While your argument is compelling," Ann said, "there is still the fact that these are living, breathing, functioning people."

"Who have no souls," Dr. King said. "*That* is what *this* debate is about, not about my family and their decisions. We know how the rest of the world looks at the soulless. And Ms. Alexander, you've seen these Copies firsthand. You've seen there's nothing in their eyes. You've also seen footage of what happens when the less tolerant come in contact with such an unnatural group. It's torture and death and destruction."

"What *you* do is the torture, death, and destruction, Dr. King," Ann Alexander said.

"We differ, Ms. Alexander. In this country, we can have opinions and express them. The facts are, there are those who have the means who can keep themselves in the best possible shape and I help *them*."

"You couldn't save the people you loved," Ann Alexander said, "but you *could* save these Terminals you take care of."

"I'm done with this interview. We have ways to save the world." There was a rustle of sound as Dr. King stood. The screen went still.

"Souls?" Abigail said. She sounded confused. The blue light from the computer made her skin seem pale.

Daniel turned. I imagined his mouth on Abigail's again and had to look away. Had Gideon kissed her, too?

"What do they mean by souls? That scares me. What else is missing from us?"

"It's what some of the Whole say makes them alive," Daniel said. "The part that connects people to some higher power." He paused. "In the real world, relationships make babies. In our case . . ."

"We were developed in a different way," I said. "And our supreme being is Dr. King."

"Just like he said," Gideon said.

"He can't give us a soul," Daniel said. "He only makes us live. The soul makes the Whole human. Some think if you don't have a soul, you're like animals."

"But," Abigail said, "we're alive. *Something* makes us live. We're not bad. We don't hurt anyone."

"Chickens or lambs or cows don't hurt anyone either. But they're all killed for food. To support the world's Replicants *and* Recipients."

This was too much to even think about. Kissing and videos and being worthless and having friends and all of it was too much. My brain felt swollen, like it needed to lose information to make my new world easier to understand.

"I'm tired," I said.

Gideon nodded. "That's part of the argument, best we can tell. We're unnatural. And with the Tonic, we appear almost lifeless."

"Soulless." Abigail's voice was a whisper, but the sound of the word stayed with me all the way back to our room and even when I put my head on my pillow and closed my eyes.

Were we even worth saving?

17

In Ms. Iverson's class, the next day, I did what I should. Sat the way I saw everyone else sitting. Watched to see how I had been and acted like I was still normal. Or was I normal now? It was hard to know.

The whole time I listened to what was said in class, I thought.

Staring at my hands, my fingernails, the fine blond hair on my arms, I couldn't help but wonder if I was worthless because I didn't have a soul. What made me have value? Who gave a soul? Parents? A creator? Dr. King?

Or ourselves?

Was Dr. King our owner? The worry made my insides cool off.

Maybe it was the not knowing that gave me no worth.

Here was my truth, the Terminals' truth, no matter if we had souls or didn't: We were the sum of our body parts.

"I thought it would be hard to see what to do," I said to Abigail at lunch. She had her head down, eating. Copying everybody like I was learning to do. There were a few whispers. Sounds of glasses being set on the wooden tabletops. And from the back, the clink of dishes being scooted away. I'd never noticed any of this before. How quiet we all were. Before we had seemed loud.

"You have to be careful," she said after a mouthful of cold asparagus soup. "Remember, we don't notice anything, but you'll get it. It's obvious. We experience nothing but fear and only when they open the doors in this room. Terminals don't care."

So that outburst of Gideon's, I knew now, put them . . . no, *us* . . . at risk. He should never have done that. He should never have reacted. He should have stayed the same, not been different.

I watched.

I watched from half-closed eyes or when I thought no one paid attention. I did it when we all lumbered toward a classroom. (We never hurried to get anywhere.) In the Dining Hall. (Where Terminals ate as if their lives depended on what they took into their bodies.) At night in our room. (Where Mary went to sleep as soon as she tucked herself under the covers.)

Changes kept coming at me. Like how the sun splashed through the stained-glass window. Sure, I had seen the colors before, but they were muted. Pale. Now they were so bright, they looked scoopable, like I might be able to hold the colors in my hands. Maybe even taste them. And the dark curtains. They were the color of blueberry juice with a red mixed in. A part of me wanted to lick at that color, try it.

Could someone with no soul appreciate beauty? Could they care? Could they memorize facts and *not* forget?

Did *I* care?

Yes.

And, I knew with that thought, I had cared *with* the Tonic. Not with my whole self because I hadn't been allowed to.

I wanted to be safe. I wanted Abigail safe. All of the Terminals. I thought this as I headed for Planting Committee, where we were now transplanting for spring (that empty promise), putting vegetables in the ground, pruning. Getting our world ready to support life that would be given away.

Opening the door that led outside, a cool breeze swept over me. The ground was wet, the grass hoping to turn green.

At first I couldn't get all the way outside. That's how fresh the wind was. I walked into the yard shielding my eyes, the light seemed so bright. It was all so new, unfolding right before me.

I walked to the greenhouse, taking the same path I had that first day when the snow was still on the ground, the cold not bothering me now as it had before. "Be the same," I whispered.

Head tucked.

Eyes forward.

Moving, but not that fast.

Listless.

Be the same.

He'll be there. Gideon.

My stomach squeezed in on itself.

The thought of lips on lips.

His lips on mine? Why would I think this?

Terminals worked around the greenhouse, weeded the old beds. I could see a few more classmates, distorted because of the Plexiglas, bent over seedlings that stretched toward the light, growing fast because of the nutrients we fed them.

I trudged toward class on the far side of campus. How had I never seen how far away the buildings were from each other? Experiencing things I knew I had experienced, but seeing them for the first time, was strange. Like déjà vu. The ground felt soft under my feet. The tires tracks of Daniel's wheelchair had filled with water. Had it rained and I not known it? And how did Daniel get everywhere before me?

The greenhouses weren't too far ahead now. Three long buildings, plastic skins for walls. A huge building farther back, where I had never been. As I got closer nerves made my arms itch.

Maybe there are others. The thought surprised me.

Did other Terminals on the committee know what Gideon and Abigail and Daniel and I knew? Were there Terminals doing what we were doing? Ones we didn't know about?

My hand went to my scar. There was pressure when I touched the wound, something I hadn't felt since the early days after the operation.

I opened the door. The smell of dirt was so strong, I closed my eyes.

Gideon said, "You're letting in cold air."

"Sorry," I said, and pulled the door to.

Gideon sat at the table, transferring tomato plants, some that had small green tomatoes on them, into bigger pots. Once we planted them—half in the greenhouse, half in the gardens—those plants would yield fruit for the rest of the year. Would he and I be here to eat it?

I hung my coat on the back of a chair and smoothed my hands down my sweats.

"You have work to do," Gideon said. He kept his eyes on his work. His voice was flat.

"What is it?"

Where was Daniel? This was a question I couldn't ask, because I wouldn't have. Tricky.

"You need to move those to the shaded area of the gazebo. You'll see where the ground has been readied. No worry of frost now. They'll be okay. Make sure you fertilize the ground first."

Gideon pointed to several containers of budding flowers in a red wagon. There was earth on the side of the wagon, a bit of rust, mud on the wheels. How had I missed all this before?

Maybe I missed things because I am soulless.

No. I missed things because of the Tonic.

Gideon said, "I'll be out soon. I have to finish here."

Where were Abigail and Daniel? Kissing somewhere?

Dragging the wagon behind me, I went outside, wind tugging at my braid that was coming loose, hand cold on the metal handle.

Don't lift your face to the sky. Don't glance at the sun. Don't watch the clouds, open your mouth, and drink in the air.

Terminals existed, yes. But we didn't what? We didn't *live.*

Checking over my shoulder, I saw Gideon, bent over his work.

It was a long walk to the gazebo. When had I seen that light, glowing outside, not far from here? The experience was fuzzy in my memory.

A few minutes later, I knelt before the turned-over ground of the flower bed. I made holes in the soft earth. The dirt was cool on my hands.

With care, I removed a tender plant, held it to my nose. The bitter smell filled me, caught in my throat. I'd smelled this before, I just

133

hadn't *felt* this pleasure. My mouth moved in the beginnings of a smile and I touched my lips with chilly fingertips. No smiling. Instead, I worked with a steady rhythm, digging in the earth, adding liquid fertilizer from the gallon jug that read COMPOST.

"Need help?"

Gideon surprised me. Had he seen me caressing the plants? He stood in front of the sun, light bursting around him. His hair moved in the wind, but I couldn't quite see his face. I shook my head no, but he knelt across the flower bed from me, taking a tray from the wagon.

"Keep them in the shaded areas," I said.

Gideon nodded.

"What's the rest of the class doing?" I asked. Now that Gideon was no longer standing in front of the sun, I could see him better. His skin was smooth and freckles ran over his cheekbones. His lips were pink. I looked back at my work. I would not think of his lips. Why had I seen Ms. Iverson and Mr. Tremmel? Why had Abigail told me about kissing Daniel? Why was I this way about Gideon?

"They're in the indoor garden. Getting vegetables in the ground. The crew's out here working up the beds."

We were silent. For the first time in my life, I felt uncomfortable with silence.

"We shouldn't be talking," Gideon said. "We never did."

"I know."

I pressed the weedy flower into the ground, pouring in a bit of the thick liquid compost (like the Tonic we drank?) over the roots, then packing the plant down tight. I moved to the next few holes. My fingers were cold. I pulled gloves from my apron pocket and put them on.

"I think people have run in the past," Gideon said.

My tongue tried to slide down my throat. "Oh?"

He said, "Keep planting in case they're watching."

My hands trembled at the possibility. The Tonic blocked out the world and some of the nerves, but it had never stopped the shaking.

I patted the ground. "What makes you think others have tried?"

They didn't succeed.

They failed.

We are still here.

"Clues."

Okay.

"Like the computers in the basement? Those videos and files were there. Just for the finding. A year ago, Adam showed me that room. Plus a couple others we hide in."

Adam? I almost remembered an Adam.

What had happened to him? Had the Illness taken him?

Gideon was silent then he said, "Do you remember way back? When we were young? The older Terminals were sort of our partners. They took care of us. Do you remember that?"

I stopped digging. The soil was so dark.

I *did* recall that time. Someone helped with my hair. An olive-skinned girl named Sarah. I closed my eyes to the memory of her gentle touch. "She was a Keeper," I said.

It was all a blur. Faint.

Gideon kept talking. "I'm not surprised if you don't. When they found other ways to control us, they did. They got rid of the buddy system. They washed our memories of a lot of it."

"Why do you remember?" A breeze picked up and a chill went through me.

"Adam wouldn't let me forget." Gideon swallowed loud enough, I heard him. "Then one day—"

I knew what was coming. "He was gone."

Gideon cleared his throat a couple of times. "Before Adam left, he

135

got me off the Tonic. He told me that was part of the escape plan and showed me the different rooms.

"Later, I went looking for whatever he hid. Since then Daniel and I have been collecting data any way we can and storing it on the computers."

"Did Adam stay for a while?" My Sarah wasn't in my brain for long.

Gideon gave a slight nod.

"He left close to when the Whole male came for you."

"That wasn't that long ago, Gideon. You said so. My Keeper left when I was little."

The plants on my side of the gazebo were in the ground. A bed of green that would change to I-didn't-know-what color. This would look nice, all in bloom. Nice was an odd thing for me to think, but I liked the idea of what would come of my work. I brushed my gloved hands together. "I'm going back." I grabbed the leftover pots, my tools, and put them in the wagon.

"I can walk with you," Gideon said. "I'm done, too."

He stood and I couldn't help but notice how slender he was. I tugged the wagon along and it clanked as it bounced over the grass.

"Let's you and me go tonight," Gideon said.

"You and I."

"Right. You and I."

"Go where?"

"There's a building I've wanted to break into for some time," he said.

"I'm not sure. Just the two of us?" I walked with my head down, but my face felt warm even in the cold afternoon air. Gideon loped a few paces ahead.

"I can't get Daniel in a window, and I don't want to go through the rooms alone."

"But . . ."

"I could lift you. You're mostly whole. You could get in the window, let me in a door or help pull me up."

"Right," I said after a long silence.

We walked on. The sky was hurt-your-eyes blue. Or was that a normal blue and hurt only the eyes of people fresh off a Tonic? I was hyperaware of Gideon, aware of the navy color of his sweats and the lightweight jacket he wore. Aware that he wanted me to be with him tonight. That his lips were pink. That he thought I was nice to look at.

Why me? Why not Abigail? He could boost her. She might be able to help him. So could Daniel, for that matter.

There was work to be done and he needed my assistance and I would do it.

"Heart and Soul," Gideon said as we got closer to the greenhouses.

"What do you mean?"

I wanted to reach out to him. Where had *that* feeling come from?

"Those astilbe we planted? They're also called Heart and Soul."

18

"Look at this," I said to Abigail. Our room was as quiet as death. Brahms had long died out. Mary was asleep. Elizabeth's made bed was still empty. I couldn't look at it without a lump forming in my throat.

I had changed my clothes to go off with Gideon. Daniel and Abigail would meet us in an hour to watch a documentary. More Dr. King stuff? I wasn't sure.

"What?" Abigail sat up, propping herself against the wall with her pillow.

I padded in the near-darkness to the side of her bed. "I can touch you," I said. "I mean, I *want* to touch Terminals now." I reached out a finger to her hand. My stomach folded over but I didn't feel like throwing up. "I'm not sick like before."

"Isn't that strange?" she asked. "I know what you mean. When I went off the Tonic, I wanted to caress everyone. Finger Esther's long, dark hair. It looks so shiny, you know? And when Elizabeth left, I wanted to hug her good-bye."

I moved to my side of the room and slipped my shoes on. Pillows tucked a shape beneath the covers. "It's so unusual that people outside here can reach out to another. That touching is part of the Whole's world."

"I saw on Interstar about these Whole babies who *hadn't* been allowed to touch. Sometimes they die. Or they grow up incomplete."

"Like us?"

Abigail shrugged. "Maybe." She settled into bed. Her voice had a smile in it. From talking? I wasn't sure. "Have you noticed other things?"

I plumped up the pillows some, trying to make them look more Terminal-like. "Give me an example."

"Well, like . . . males?"

My neck prickled with warmth.

"Do you want to press to them the way Ms. Iverson and Mr. Tremmel did in the hallway?" Abigail said.

"Of course not."

"Just wait," Abigail said, like she offered me a promise of good things. She spoke with a sigh. "The next thing you know, they're all going to appear attractive."

Gideon in the sun. Hair moving in that slight wind. Was he . . . attractive?

Him telling me I was nice to look at.

Was he nice to look at?

I thought so. Yes. I nodded at no one.

"They're still Terminals to me. Not just plain males," I said, hoping the Gideon memory didn't seep into my words. I finished dressing, pulling on a dark knit cap to hide my hair.

"Shiloh."

The voice came from our doorway and I whirled around. Across from where I stood, Abigail gasped, pulling her covers to her chin.

"I'm here."

"Gideon?" I hurried across the floor though my knees felt like they had soaked in vinegar and gone soft. "What are you doing here?" Was this my dream, come to life? Something lodged near my lung.

He stepped into our room and Abigail said, "You get caught in here, with Shiloh dressed like that, and we are all done. Everything we've worked for will be wasted." Her tone could have diced vegetables.

"I didn't want her to walk alone," Gideon said. He was a shadow. In the dim of evening, his face seemed full of holes.

"I've walked alone before," I said. I rubbed my arms to calm myself.

"We're going a different way," he said.

"You're taking too many risks," Abigail said.

"Abigail, I won't jeopardize the Cause."

She was on her feet now. She raised her hand to point at him. "You already have. More than once."

Gideon said, "We'll meet you in an hour."

She didn't answer.

The breeze from that afternoon had picked up to a strong wind that blew from the north.

"What you did was dangerous," I said.

Gideon turned, leaned till he was close to my face. "Don't judge me," he said. His breath smelled of spearmint.

I swallowed, surprised—another new emotion. "I wasn't," I said. Something hot bubbled up the back of my throat. My eyes narrowed. Geez, without the Tonic, I couldn't control anything, especially not the way I felt. "I was stating a fact."

Gideon didn't answer. The pull to obey tugged against the desire to leave Gideon to do this work alone. Neither of us spoke now, but walked down the side of the building, sticking to the shadows.

I tucked my head into my jacket, hands into the pockets. The chill made me curl up. When we Terminals stayed in the warmth of the building, our lives were easy.

Why had I thought that? It wasn't true at all. Our lives were not even our own. There was nothing easy about that. The realization I still wanted to obey held as much bite as the air.

Gideon walked in front of me, moving forward in the dark like he knew the way well.

"You do this outside sneaking a lot?"

He grunted.

"Does that mean yes?"

He stopped and turned to face me. I ran right into him. He was at least six inches taller. I'd never noticed before. The scales were falling from my eyes. "It means we have to be quiet until we get across the campus," he said. "We have to be quiet out here. Voices carry in the dark. There are cameras to avoid."

"Outside?"

Gideon's words floated back to me. "We figure it's how they knew you and Abigail scaled the wall." He marched on, taking such large steps that I almost had to jog to keep up. The speed was difficult but I wouldn't complain. He'd asked me to come along. I needed to make myself do whatever needed to be done. "There are cameras everywhere."

We raced across campus, moving from tree to tree until the last distance to be covered was a large expanse of ground. I panted, trying to bring in enough oxygen.

"I'll go first," Gideon said when we stopped under a downy hawthorn. "Keep low as you run. We're headed to the hospital."

No Terminal, not one, was allowed in that building. Dr. King had an office there—that was the rumor. And things happened there.

Across the campus. Suitcase in hand.

Someone near.

People waiting.

The whiteness of the room.

Blinding light.

This was why I was anxious. Thinking too much. I gulped in the cold night air.

"You okay?" Gideon asked. He stepped closer like he wanted to see my face in the sliver-moon's light.

"Yes. I just can't go as fast." My mouth wanted to say, *We can't go there. We can't.* But I wouldn't be afraid.

Gideon nodded. He rested his hand on my arm. "We'll wait till you catch your breath."

The warmth of his fingers seeped through my sweatshirt. Why wasn't he colder? I concentrated on calming myself, ignoring the bit of pain in my side and the fear of going into this strictly off-limits building. There. My chest wasn't so tight. Would I ever get used to living with just one lung? A sudden flame burned through my stomach. Why did I have to give a part of me away without choosing to?

"Ready?" Gideon said.

"Yes."

"Leave thirty seconds after I do. Meet me in the blacker parts near the buildings. East side. At the back."

I could do that. I'd hiked all over this campus, had memorized the position of trees and bushes, where fountains and decorative walls stood. Though I always kept my distance from this place, I knew where Gideon wanted me to go.

The moon was swallowed whole by the clouds and Gideon took off running. He moved fast. "Just keep low" was the last bit of advice he gave me, the words thin as a spirit.

I counted, slower than when the doors in the dining hall opened. At thirty I stepped from the shadow of the tree and into the openness of the quad.

Overhead, the moon sat sideways, visible again, like it had rolled back on its hip for a rest. Pale almost-not-there light, fell on me. I was a target. Anyone looking into the courtyard could see who I was.

"Hey, look! There's Shiloh," I imagined someone saying.

And then the response, "What's she doing out there?"

I had seen the flicking red light, and seen the shape. What kept others from looking as I had?

That run was like being naked with everyone at Haven Hospital & Halls watching. Eyes pierced me between the shoulder blades, studied my scar, accused me of breaking rules. I'd never felt so vulnerable.

Except the day of my operation when they put that mask over my face.

I've changed my mind.

A bit of red light (well!) blinked once, then was gone. Not from my memory. For real.

Gideon.

I reached the building and the darkness.

"Gideon?"

No answer.

I moved a hand out, touching the roughness of bricks. The wind nipped at my skin. I strained to see anything in the shadows. Then I worked along, my back to the building. It felt as though someone had a tight hold on my chest from the inside.

"Hello?" Where was Gideon? Disappeared into the earth?

Right there, all hollow-faced, skeletal in the dark.

"Are you okay?" Gideon touched my shoulder. When he moved, I still felt that weight, pressing into my skin.

I covered my mouth and nose to warm the air going into my body. Bending over seemed to help a little, so I did, curling down toward my knees.

"Shiloh?"

I nodded an answer. "Show me what we need to do," I said. "I want to go back to bed. I've got to sleep. I want to be ready for Ms. Iverson's classes tomorrow."

"This side of the building," he said.

"Right."

We started again, the wind whistling close by, like it knew we were there and meant to drive us away. I kept my mouth covered. My fingers felt like slivers of cold metal.

Gideon said, "All we have to do is go in through that window." He pointed up. Above us was a row of muddy-colored glass. Concrete sills glowed pale in the weak moonlight. These were way too high to climb into unless Gideon had been eight feet tall.

"You'll never make it," I said.

"But you can. I'll boost you."

"Me?" I shook my head. "I don't know how."

His clothing rustled and I imagined Gideon had shrugged. "Then you get comfortable on that ledge and pull me up behind you."

I hesitated. "I'm not sure I can do that. I'm not sure I'm strong enough."

"Of course you can, Shiloh. You've done this before. When you and Abigail went up the wall. That was a lot higher than where we are now."

I cleared my throat, which felt as cold as my fingers for some reason. "Okay. I'll try."

The wind stilled and I heard Gideon breathing.

"You okay with me touching you now?"

"What?"

"I told you I wouldn't touch you till you asked."

"I see." I changed my tone of voice, waggled my head from side to side. "Will you touch me, Gideon? Help me up?" My heart flip-flopped.

"Sure," Gideon said. "I'll help you. Put your foot in my hand. Balance against me."

Everything we did confused me. Every command was opposite to what Terminals do. Still, I stepped into his hand and Gideon lifted me into the air.

"Let the wall help you balance. Like before with Abigail."

You can do that, Shiloh.

Touch me, Gideon.

Touch me.

The brick was rough under my hands, cold, but I was high enough to see into the window. I pushed against the glass that was colder than the wall. It slid apart and I pushed again and again until there was room for me to get through.

"It's open." My heart pounded in my face, in my eyes. Warm air billowed out on me and my skin stung.

"Can you balance on the sill, then pull me up?"

"Why not?" I leaned in through the opening, my aching hands holding my weight. *Pull up your legs, both of them. Swing around. Watch it! Careful!*

"Careful," Gideon said.

Somehow I got into position—half in, half out of the building—and I leaned for Gideon, the sill cutting me in half.

"Take my hand," I said, waving my arms so he could catch hold in the darkness. "And hurry. I'm balancing on my stomach. This hurts."

Gideon's hand caught one of mine, then the other. He grabbed my wrists, locking on tight.

"Pull," he said.

I did and the frame of the window ground into my stomach. When I tugged on Gideon, I slipped and then my ribs were being separated by metal and concrete. My scar burned like I'd pressed into a flame on the stove.

"Come on!" I almost didn't get the words out.

Then, Gideon and I were face-to-face. He exhaled on my cheeks, on my lips. The memory of being sick tried to make me dizzy but I wouldn't let it.

"You've got to move, Shiloh, or I can't get in."

That made sense. "Where?" I tried to slide over, but the window was only so big.

"Drop in the building."

"Are you serious?"

"Yes." Now Gideon sounded winded. "Drop."

"There might be someone waiting. This might not even be a room." I kept my balance, worked not to slip into the nothingness behind me.

"I'm losing my grip and we're going to be stuck. You in there, me out here."

"But what if Dr. King's here?"

"Shiloh!"

I slid down the wall, toes reaching for something. Then I let go, landing on . . . what? A bed? I gasped. Was there someone in it? Would I wake him? Another step, this one sideways. No, I was on a sofa. What a relief! Above me, Gideon filled the window.

"Ouch."

"What?" Gideon asked. He slid down the wall beside me. He closed the pane of glass.

I shook my head though I was sure he couldn't see me. Was the skin gone from my hands and arms? And my ribs and stomach—maybe a "fold here" line had been etched into the flesh.

"Careful," Gideon said. His fingers were warm. "Step down."

I followed, crunching my hand into a ball. He squeezed my fist, tugged me after him, kept ahold though there wasn't much to hold on to.

Touch me, Gideon.

"Adam used to come in here plenty," Gideon said. "He knew all about this place. He told me about it." He flipped on a flashlight (a gift from Adam that Gideon kept hidden, stealing batteries to keep it alive).

The room smelled soft, flowery, with the strange odor behind that reminded me of being little.

The Infirmary was in the front of this building. I knew that from when I'd been sick. Maybe that was the part of the memory?

We were in a room, not too large, that looked like an office. The flashlight bounced around the walls. A few chairs, a coffee table spread with magazines. Where was Dr. King's office in relation to the Infirmary? In relation to where we stood now? An electric shock ran down my spine. The fear felt like it went out my hair.

Gideon reached for a magazine. On the cover was the woman who looked like Claudia and the title, A BRAND-NEW YOU.

The desk was large. So big, it seemed to take up the width of the room. Pictures of the Whole, all smiling, lined one wall. Bookshelves lined another.

"What are you looking for?" I asked.

Gideon shrugged, tried a few desk drawers, but came up empty-handed. "Maybe this is a consultation room," he said. "Maybe people come here after they've seen us and talk about making their own Genetic Copies."

There was nothing to say.

19

If Gideon and I were caught, what would happen?

Isolation for sure.

Anything more?

Would they use us up? Give our parts away to the highest bidder? I wouldn't think of that. I'd just walk without sound, hoping we'd get what we needed so we could meet up with Abigail and Daniel.

Abigail.

For some reason I missed her.

We stepped into the hall that glowed with almost-not-there lighting. Gideon snapped off the flashlight.

"I'll leave the door unlocked in case we want to crawl back out that window." Gideon stood so close, I could smell the soap he used to wash with. "Can I still touch you, Shiloh?"

"Yes." My voice came out a whisper, a sudden thrill running all over my body. "Yes, sure," I said, louder. "I'm okay with that."

Gideon took my hand in his and gave me a real smile—the first I had ever seen from him, then led me down the hall.

His hand was different from Abigail's. Not as soft. Not as tiny.

I felt his skin under my fingertips.

"Look," he said.

Up ahead was light, a thin strip. Like when I first saw the place I would meet Gideon and Abigail. How long ago had I thought I'd teach them a thing or two? Three days? Three weeks? It felt like years.

"Do they work all night, too?"

He turned to me, but didn't lose my hand. "What do you remember about your operation?"

"What do you mean?"

Gideon crept forward, letting the blind flashlight lead the way. "Anything you can recall."

I remembered. "There were people."

"Doctors? Nurses?"

I nodded. Maybe. "Someone put the mask over my face." The memory was foggy, not as clear as my dreams.

"Was the operation at night?"

I closed my eyes.

"The room was bright."

The light ahead was unchanging.

"I've seen Dr. King enter the building on the north side," Gideon said. His fingers laced with mine. "Maybe that's where the operating rooms are."

"This is where they operate on us?"

"Yes, Shiloh."

"Who?"

"Who operates? Dr. King, mostly. He has a few assistants. Maybe there's someone we know here."

I cleared my throat. "Are you thinking of Elizabeth? Or Isaac?"

Gideon looked at me. "We don't know what all goes on in this building. Or who's here. For sure there's the Infirmary. Like I said, they do operations here. Adam told me that. And anyone can look at the outside and see it's huge. I just wanted to see for myself."

"That's dangerous," I said.

"Sure," Gideon said, "what we're doing is deadly. But doing nothing kills us, too. Maybe when we get out of here we can use your memory, and you can tell everyone what's going on in here. We know your family connections will help."

As soon as the words came out of his mouth, I knew Gideon was right.

"I asked Dr. King about this building," Gideon said. "Asked him what goes on here. He told me it's just the Infirmary and a few offices. But then he made me take a triple dose of Tonic. That was a long time ago."

"Why are we here?" I asked.

"Because he thinks we're stupid."

I didn't answer.

Ahead were double doors. The kind that swing both ways.

Gideon stopped, his head lowered.

He didn't move, just stood with his head bowed, my hand loose in his. "I miss Adam," he said.

I understood it now, that missing someone. The ache of it. That loss.

He let out a sigh. "Let's just hurry. We can't stand around talking." He pulled me closer and I bumped into him. The strip of light grew brighter as we neared.

Was Dr. King behind the door up ahead? Did he know we were in the building? Did he watch us?

"I can't hear anything." Gideon looked at me. In the dimness of that hall his eyes seemed warm. What if I put my arms around him? If I put my lips to his? Touched his cheek with a fingertip? I shouldn't think any of this.

"Your eyes might be too blue," I said. I took a step forward.

"Are they?" Gideon tugged me closer.

"Maybe."

"The Whole think the eyes are the window to the soul."

I touched my throat, and my fingertips were cold as bullets. "But we don't . . ."

Gideon nodded. "I know."

This time when I touched his palm the warmth there soothed me. Gideon's hand wrapped around mine and it was like he pulled all the air from my body.

I had never been touched like this. I mean, yes. He had touched me. And I had yelled at him. And Abigail, too. But this was different. I'd never felt this way. Not ever that I could remember.

"Ready?"

He stood close now. So close that when I looked up at him, I knew I'd look right into his eyes. If he had a soul, would I see it? And what was it that Ms. Iverson had done? Stood on tiptoe to get closer to Mr. Tremmel.

"Ready." My answer was a whisper.

Gideon pushed with his shoulder against the door, opening it until he could see into the room beyond. "It's an empty hall," he said.

All that worry for nothing?

I clasped his hand in both of mine, brought it to my mouth, warming my fingers some in his.

150

No wonder they never wanted us to touch. Terminals would fight to know this feeling.

We crept into the hall that was lit by a cord of light that ran near the baseboard. There was a reflection of creamy yellow in the polished floor. Both walls were lined with windowless doors. Beads of light, just drops really, hung from the ceiling.

"What is this?"

"Look and see," my mouth said, and I wasn't even sure where those words had come from. Was I curious? No! Curiosity killed the Terminal. I wanted to hurry and get out of here. I wasn't interested in anything but climbing back in bed and pulling the covers over my head.

And in holding Gideon's warm hand. In standing near him.

Gideon grabbed the first doorknob we came to. I walked so close, I was almost on his heels. I could have tripped over him. He pushed the door open.

The space was dark. Pitch-black.

"Hold on," Gideon said, slipping into the room and pulling me behind him. "Don't let the door shut or we may get locked in here."

That wouldn't do. "Okay," I said. I stayed by the entrance.

The flashlight snapped on. Stainless-steel refrigerators ran along one wall. Cabinets and countertops were on the opposite side of the room. Was this a kitchen? Where was the stove?

Gideon did something with the doorknob, and allowed the door to close all the way.

"Wait!" I said, the word coming out in a panic.

"It's okay. I made sure we could get out. Find a light switch. And let's be quick about this."

I ran a slow hand over the wall next to the entrance and found two switches. "Got it," I said.

"Turn it on."

"I . . . I don't want to."

"Shiloh." Gideon sounded frustrated. "We have to hurry."

"I know. But I'm scared."

Gideon put his arm around my shoulder and squeezed me closer. "Me, too," he said, whispering. The words went into my hair. I heard him swallow. Saw him squeeze his eyes closed. "But we need this information for the outside world. And we need to get back to Abigail and Daniel."

"Right." Still I hesitated. Then I flipped on the light. I peeked out at the room. Only the countertops were illuminated.

The refrigerators gleamed in the semidarkness. Not one fingerprint. The fronts seemed to have been buffed. I followed Gideon, raised my hand, and opened the first appliance. A strong, almost sour smell rushed out with the cold air, turning my stomach.

I saw trays. Large and small trays. Covered with plastic wrap.

"Parts." Gideon's voice came from far away, somewhere near the ceiling.

I recognized the hands first.

Two in each small tray.

Colorless.

Were those noses? Skin? What was that? Three jars of eyes?

"Leftover pieces," he said. "To be disposed of. Maybe. Or used in some kind of research."

In slow motion, I turned. Gideon stood right there beside me.

How could he float? And then the words *leftover pieces*. I heard the opening and closing of doors.

"These *all* hold parts. Tissue. Joints and limbs. Organs. Maybe the Recipients to these parts are dead." Gideon sounded shaky.

"Why do you say that?" My mouth was doing that moving-on-its-own thing. How had the words come from me? I could taste the smell from the fridge.

Gideon peered over my shoulder, then pulled me back so he could shut the door. The room fell into semidarkness again. His grip was too tight.

"I don't know. But I would think you'd have to keep transplant tissue alive in some way. Not cold like this."

I swallowed. His eyes were as blue as the painful sky had been today.

"Who is it? Who are they?" A swarm of bees tumbled in my chest. "Could this be Elizabeth? Or Isaac?"

"You can't ask that," Gideon said. "Let's go."

"Could it?" My heart battered at my ribs. I pulled the refrigerator door open. Was she in here? My roommate? I heaved and clasped my hand over my mouth.

"You can't think that, Shiloh. We have to leave. Now."

Nothing looked familiar in these parts. Nothing looked like Elizabeth. I pushed the door shut. Stepped to the next refrigerator, opened it.

"No," I said. "No."

There were several jugs labeled COMPOST. Gallon jugs. The kind I fed plants from.

Were these? Were these bits and pieces? Ground-up parts?

Gideon pushed the refrigerator shut. "We're going."

We flipped off the lights, opened the door leading to the hall, then went to the next room. Again, it was dark. Again Gideon ran the flashlight around the room.

Body parts.

Elizabeth.

Don't think of her.

Isaac.

Ground into fertilizer.

In the next room, the walls were almost bare, but this time, in the middle, was a bed with rails on one side. There was equipment everywhere—a large light was centered over the bed, with a neck that allowed the bulb to move closer to or farther away from whatever might be lying there.

Pain hit me like a bat, like when I tried to clean the Tonic from my body. I dropped to one knee. "Ow ow ow."

"What Shiloh?"

"The headache. It's back."

He cupped my face, but the pain was so bad, I could hardly feel his touch.

"Shiloh," he said.

I couldn't move.

"Look at me."

"Can't."

"Pay attention to what I tell you."

I tried to concentrate on Gideon. I felt the warmth of his palms on my cheeks. "It's a memory," he said. "It's happened to me a couple times when I wind up in places I shouldn't be. Knocked me on my back. Do you hear me? It's only a memory."

A memory.

Yes.

I scrunched my forehead. "I've been here," I said. "I've been on that table."

I've changed my mind.

She looks too much like my daughter.

For Victoria.

Gideon wrapped his arm around me, pulled me to my feet. He held me so close, I felt his body all down the side of my body. My head pounded.

I was exhausted from what I had seen. From what I remembered.

154

"There's a basement exit," Gideon said as we rushed to get back to everyone else. "I noticed it the other day."

I could almost not see. I stumbled as he flicked out the light.

We prowled around, my eyes blurred more than normal in the dark, until we found an EXIT sign and stairs leading down a floor. The farther we moved from the room, from the memory, the less intense the headache became, until all the pain was gone.

"More rooms to explore here," I said.

Gideon slowed. "Are you up to it?"

"I don't want to ever come back here," I said. "Let's do it now. Get it over with." Where was Elizabeth? Had my heart failed me?

They were recovery rooms. That's what a posted sign said. One door stood open. Thin light fell out into the hall.

"We'll check there," Gideon said.

He caught my hand again. My skin felt almost hot from his touch. Too many thoughts ran through my head. Dr. King and Elizabeth. Mr. Tremmel and Ms. Iverson. Abigail pressing her lips to Daniel's. And I would dream forever of those body parts.

"Hurry," I said. The hairs on my arms stood up. Panic swirled through me.

In the dimness of the hall, I saw Gideon nod. We crept to the door. Peeked in.

I saw someone, an older male, lying on the bed, tubes and wires, monitors and machines hooked up to him.

Gideon took a step forward, dropping my hand. He motioned me back. My pulse quickened. Three steps into the room. Pause. Turn. Back away. Silence roared in my ears.

I could see the form on the bed clearly now. I staggered. An older Gideon.

My Gideon stepped back next to me. He moved so fast, I thought for sure my arm would be separated from my shoulder.

Down the hall. Down another set of stairs. Farther away. Farther.

"Wait," I said. My lips tingled. "Slow down. Please."

Ahead of us, the way out.

"Wait," I said, "that was you."

Gideon shook his head. "No," he said. "It was Adam." Tears streamed down his face.

"That was you." I was panting. "An older you."

But Gideon never stopped.

HAVEN
HOSPITAL & HALLS
Where You Matter
Established 2020

Note to all Staff

We are getting closer to the problem. Thanks to those who have stepped forward and helped in this investigation. You will be compensated.

Please be aware of unusual movement at night.

All reports need to be made to school officials.

Do not try to stop any uprising on your own, as this could be dangerous.

I carry my prepared suitcase.

We walk out the back door.

Across the lawn. I could turn around and run back to Abigail. Run to safety. To our room.

Keys out. Jangling. My mouth full of fear.

Two people ahead.

They don't speak.

I see the table. There's a woman and an older man and Dr. King. He's dressed like a surgeon.

"Don't struggle." He puts the mask over my face.

But I fight. I slap at his hands, scratch at a Nurse. Kick the tray of surgical instruments.

"Count back from a hundred, Shiloh," he says, and holds my head still. His grip is tight. Someone straps my feet and hands down.

And there is a voice.

That voice.

I try to look at her.

The one on the table. It's me on the table.

"I've changed my mind. She looks too much like my daughter."

"You paid for it."

"I know, but . . ."

A man's voice now. "For Victoria, Ann. We're doing it for Victoria."

"Yes, I know. But it may not work."

"Breathe, Shiloh."

"We have to keep Victoria alive."

"Just this once."

"Promise me, never again."

"I promise."

"Count back from a hundred."

"It isn't human," Dr. King says. "It's made by me, not created by you."

I don't breathe until I have to.

20

Eyes in jars watched me. A rush of cold poured through my bones. When my feet hit the carpeted floor, I awoke.

"What is it, Shiloh?" Abigail asked.

Outside, the sky turned the color of early morning.

"Sorry," I said. "Sorry." I climbed back into bed.

"Dreaming?"

"I don't think so." I shook my head.

"You screamed."

"It was real, I think. A memory. Not a dream." I still felt the mask on my face, the straps that had held me down.

160

Abigail went silent. She cleared her throat. When she spoke, her voice wavered a bit. "The Tonic keeps the truth of our operations away. I remember bits of mine, too. Like—" Again she cleared her throat. "—like how Dr. King said my arm wasn't mine. That the arm could be used for the Recipient who'd been crushed in an accident. How he told someone that the surgery wouldn't leave even a bit of a scar. Not one at all."

Neither of us spoke. And then, "I'm scared," I whispered. "I'm scared, Abigail. Last night was too real."

"Me, too," she said. I saw her swallow, like the pause might give her a bit of strength. "That's why we fight. So we can get out of here. Be free. And we don't have to be afraid anymore."

Without the Tonic, school became exciting. I loved classes (though I was sometimes tired), loved learning. I fell into gathering facts. Not even bad dreams—or awful memories—or body parts—could take away the joy of stuffing information into my brain.

English was my favorite time. I wanted to memorize every quote, and with the Tonic gone it felt like my brain worked smoother, remembered more. Ms. Iverson had the walls decorated with posters telling us to READ! There were pictures of famous authors—some who are Terminals like us. Just looking at all those writers made my heart quiet down, made me almost forget Dr. King, the refrigerators in the back building, the older Gideon. I felt wide-eyed as I waited for Ms. Iverson to speak about literature each day.

"John Steinbeck," Ms. Iverson said, "was a Terminal himself." His photo in the book didn't show he looked different. But Terminals could lose any body part, not just something above the shoulders.

Ms. Iverson pressed the paperback to her chest like this book meant something to her. Could that be? Could we care for more than each other? Even for books? "He writes of Terminals in *Of Mice and Men*. So far, we've met several. Who are they?"

"Candy," Matthew said. "He's missing the hand." Matthew held up both his arms that ended in pinkish stubs right above the elbows. "Plus he's old and weathered."

I'd seen Matthew almost every day of our lives, and of course since this operation, but today, when he held his arms up, I gasped.

"Good," Ms. Iverson said. "Who else?"

What was left of Matthew's arms looked so raw, a powerful sensation flooded through me, one I didn't recognize, and I thought I'd have to stand, walk out, maybe even get to the bathroom.

"Curley. He's a Terminal in ways that aren't the same as what happens to us." This was Jeremiah speaking. I'd never realized just how dark and shiny his hair was. "You know, his handicap is in his head—in his meanness."

"I'm proud of you for keeping up with your Braille, Jeremiah. I know this is new to you. But you're doing terrific." Ms. Iverson nodded and stepped away from her desk.

"And what about Lennie?" she asked. "Tell me more about him."

Matthew spoke again. "Lennie represents the world. We may be Terminal, but all of us here are smart. We have big goals."

"Like Gideon said the other day," I said, "maybe one of us will change our futures."

Ms. Iverson glanced at me.

"You remember that, Shiloh?" she asked. "You remember Gideon talking about those things?"

"Umm." I parted my lips. Nodded.

"Have you told anyone what Gideon said?"

"No."

In the front of the classroom, Daniel scowled. Gideon seemed not to care. I could see his profile. His face didn't change at all.

"It's best *not* to say anything," Ms. Iverson said. "It's best for everyone."

"Yes. All right."

"Other comments," Ms. Iverson said.

Daniel spoke. "The world doesn't think. The Whole are like Lennie."

I could almost hear him say, *If we want cures, we're going to have to come up with them ourselves.* Like he did when the four of us met together.

"Interesting idea, Daniel. Let's keep reading."

Before, I was jumpy and afraid when the doors to the dining room opened in their slow way and Principal Harrison and Dr. King walked in carrying someone's files. Or if Terminals came too close. Or if I didn't eat everything on my plate. Or if I remembered something I shouldn't, or dreamed what I wasn't allowed to dream.

The fear changed. Became controllable. Like being almost caught by Ms. Iverson for remembering. Heart-pounding for the moment and then gone. The anxiety didn't linger. The strange thing was I hadn't known I was afraid until the fear was gone. I was used to one thing, so used to it, I didn't know a difference until the burden was removed.

Sitting there in class, only a few Terminals *knowing,* I thought of Principal Harrison and Dr. King. I saw them in a different way. Before, I thought they protected me. Now, they were the enemy. It was like *I* had been the Recipient of some new body part. They didn't care about us here. Not one of the Whole did.

How much money did they make off us? What were Daniel's legs worth? How much had Abigail's arm gotten them? What had my lung cost? I squeezed my pencil until it snapped in half.

Ms. Iverson set the book on her desk. "So what I want is an essay today. Just two hundred and fifty words. I want it on how you are different from Lennie. I want this essay on what Daniel said—how you listen to each other."

A nod here or there.

"Do you need another pencil, Shiloh?" Ms. Iverson asked.

I clasped my hands together until they hurt. Shook my head no. Then I pulled out paper and, using the nub of the pencil, started an essay that proved I knew nothing when really I was starting to discover everything.

That night, essay done and waiting in my folder, I changed into the clothes we would sneak around the buildings in. In her corner of the room, Abigail did, too.

"I hope we learn something tonight," I said. My whisper seemed loud in the room, not at all cottony like I hoped for. As the Tonic left us our hearing got better. I wasn't used to this yet.

"Shhh!" Abigail said.

From outside our room, I heard a sound. Someone?

Yes! A gruff voice.

"Bed," Abigail said.

I slowed long enough to kick my just-put-on shoes into the closet and then I climbed into bed, pulling the covers to my neck and turning my back to the door.

There was the low murmur of voices. Ms. Iverson. She sounded upset. What was she doing awake at this hour? And who was with her? Mr. Tremmel again? Gosh, I hoped not.

But these weren't happy voices. This sounded like an argument.

Abigail settled in bed as our door swung open.

A flashlight beam moved across the room. I saw it reflect off the window. Saw the shadow of two people in the doorway, mirrored in the glass. I heard Ms. Iverson say, "They're asleep, I tell you."

Dr. King's voice—what was he doing here?—followed the light.

Blood pounded through my veins. In my ears, low and deep. Act normal, I thought. Fake I was asleep. That I had taken the Tonic. That I wasn't changed. Regular, deep breaths.

What would I do if he came to my bed, pulled back the covers, and saw me in my street clothes? I gasped in a small bit of air.

"I told you," he said, "I thought I should check this room and I always go with my instincts."

"And I told you," Ms. Iverson said, "they're asleep. Look at them."

Dr. King stood at the foot of Elizabeth's empty bed. I could see him in the window, could tell from his voice where he was. "We'll have a new Terminal for this bed soon," he said.

What?

Oh, Elizabeth.

Elizabeth wasn't coming back.

I fought myself to breathe in a regular pattern. Now he stood at Mary's bed. He moved to Abigail's. What was she doing? Where was my nightgown? Had I folded it? It wasn't under my pillow. Was it on the floor?

How long would I be in Isolation for this?

It was then that Mary screamed, a bloodcurdling scream, that caused the hair on the back of my neck to stand up. It went on forever, so loud that the whole of Haven Hospital & Halls should have awakened. Except Terminals who were so drugged, they slept through anything.

Ms. Iverson ran to her. Dr. King swung the flashlight around the room like the cry had startled him, too.

"Mary, Mary. Shhh."

"The light," Mary said. She thrashed in bed. "The light."

"Turn it off," Ms. Iverson said.

Part of me wanted to sit up, but I didn't move. I would have slept through Mary's nightmare like she always slept through mine.

"I told you we would bother them," Ms. Iverson said. She sounded angry.

Dr. King sighed. "You're right."

The flashlight died.

Ms. Iverson made soothing noises. It took only a moment to quiet Mary.

Every muscle in my body was rigid. Would they never leave? *Just concentrate,* I thought. *Think yourself to sleep.*

Then next to my ear came Dr. King's voice.

"I'm watching you all," he said.

21

Even after they were gone, and had been gone for a while, neither Abigail nor I said anything. I heard the clock dong two more times before I slipped out of bed.

"What are you doing?" Abigail asked.

I pulled my shirt off. "I'm going to sleep. Really this time. That was too close." My whole body felt like it tried to tremble free of my skin.

Abigail crept over to me, crawling.

"We have plans for tonight," she said. "And the males need to know what's happened."

The light that came from the hall was shadowed by my bed and where we crouched near the floor.

"There's always a price for freedom," Abigail said.

"They'll make us pay," I said.

"Everyone pays. They always have. We've seen it on the computer.

Looking through the Histories. Abraham Lincoln, Martin Luther King, Gandhi, Joan of Arc, even John Steinbeck."

"I don't want to be punished." My voice cracked. "I don't want to die."

Abigail didn't say anything for what seemed a forever. When she opened her mouth I thought sure she'd say, *I don't either*. But she didn't. "You're going to die, Shiloh. You stay here, you die. Part by part, piece by piece. Only we can save us. Only we can be our heroes."

With the wax of the Tonic removed, I felt what maybe the Whole felt. Fear, yes. But, there was a bit of a promise, too. Not just the empty words I had thought about hope before. More than that. The chance *we* had to make a difference.

"I'm scared," I said.

"Me, too," Abigail said. "Me, too, Shiloh."

It took us longer than usual in the halls. Every sound, every crack or creak, made us hesitate. When we got to the main corridor, it was as huge and open as it had been that first night I'd left. But tonight, with Dr. King's voice in my ear, it seemed more dangerous. I gripped Abigail's hand in mine.

"We do this," she said, "for all the Terminals."

For us, I thought.

We *had* to succeed now. They knew something about what we were doing.

We jogged all the way to the basement. Quiet as spirits. We flung open the door to the closet of a room we met in.

"What took so long?" Daniel said. "You're more than an hour late."

I didn't even blink before saying, "He knows."

"What?"

"Who?"

Daniel and Gideon spoke at once, Daniel grasping the wheels to his chair, Gideon rising to his feet.

"Dr. King."

The door clicked shut behind us.

"Tell us," Daniel said.

Even at this horrible time, I couldn't keep my mind on track. Not with Gideon here. I thought of holding his hand. Him touching my face.

"He came to our room tonight," Abigail said. The walls seemed to meet each other at the ceiling. "We had just changed our clothes to come here. We were moments from leaving. If we had been any faster, he would have caught us in the corridor or gone from our beds."

I hadn't realized how close we were to getting caught. My muscles tightened with the understanding.

"He came close to me. If I had been taking the Tonic, I might have fallen from the bed from dizziness," I said. "And told me he's watching us all."

Daniel backed his wheelchair up a little. "What did *you* say?" His eyebrows were together, his face tight.

"Nothing," I said. There was an awful taste in my mouth. "I pretended to sleep."

Gideon sat. The computer screen illuminated his face. He let out a long sigh, like he was tired.

"One of us has given ourselves away." Daniel looked at me. "What have you done, Shiloh? Dr. King spoke to you."

"I . . . I don't know." Why *had* he come to me? Was it my comment in class today? My watching the other Terminals? Had someone seen me sniff the sunshine this afternoon? My every move was suspect. Had I put us all at risk? I felt sick.

"We do things," Abigail said. "In the beginning when we're coming off the drugs, we make mistakes. This isn't her fault." She cleared her throat. "Dr. King said he was watching us *all*. That means he knows about more than one of us."

My heart felt like a fist, beating out slow, dark thumps. Dr. King *had* spoken to me, not to anyone else.

He knew something about *me*.

What had I done wrong? What had given me away? And what would happen to me now?

The fist settled in my gut. "If they know," I said, "I'm the next one gone. That's how it works, right?"

Gideon shook his head but Daniel answered. "You're used when they need you. You may get Isolation, but they'll not hurt you. You're too important. You're worth a lot of money to them."

"I can't see them taking you for no reason," Gideon said. "And anyway, Shiloh, if something happened to you, the world would know."

"I don't understand."

"Your Whole connection has made a lot of noise about you, and the world is aware. It makes sense. Dr. King threatens you because you're a pawn."

"Something must have happened during your operation." This was Daniel.

I've changed my mind.

"Like what?"

"We don't know for sure. As we've reviewed different videos, there's been talk of Replicant complications."

She looks too much like my daughter. An unsettled feeling grew.

Gideon said, "Something bad. Why did they take only one lung? Your Recipient had several operations lined up."

"Enough that I wouldn't be here now?"

He nodded. "Some were serious, too. Your recipient needed you."

"She looks too much like my daughter."

"What?" Abigail asked.

I hadn't meant for the words to come out. "That's what she said."

"Who?"

"The little female's mom. Ann. I . . . I thought it was a dream. I thought it was because of the operation."

For Victoria, Ann. We're doing it for Victoria.

Just this once?

Yes. Just this once.

And if it doesn't save her . . . if we don't see a marked improvement?

Right.

I saw the bright light. Struggled with people holding me down. Heard the voices.

I've changed my mind. She looks too much like my daughter.

"Ann didn't want to do the operation. But two males talked her into at least part of the procedure."

You paid for it.

"The *it* was me. Dr. King called me 'it.' He told her I had been paid for." I closed my eyes as the memory unfolded more clear than ever before. "They would operate only one time. She made them promise."

"The female's kept her promise. She's fighting for you. Nothing will happen to you until she loses the court battles she's started to get you free from here."

"What happened to the female . . . the Recipient?" The room was too cold and I wished I had brought my jacket from Planting Committee.

"There was a failure. In one interview, the male who came to get you said operation orders were halted when it was obvious that it wasn't going to work. The Recipient is now deceased."

170

"She died?"

"We think so, Shiloh," Gideon said. "We're not sure if she—"

"The Recipient was named Victoria," I said.

No one said anything and then, "We're not sure if she died on the table or later," Gideon said. "We just know all operations were concluded."

"So Dr. King doesn't have a one hundred percent success rate," Abigail said.

"What doctor does?" Daniel asked.

"They could have parted me out," I said, "but they let me live." I was theirs to use. A Duplicate, a Terminal with no soul.

"Let's go to bed," Abigail said. "Pretend like we know nothing just for tonight."

"I agree," I said. The information was overwhelming.

"We can't hide now," Daniel said. "They know something about Shiloh, for sure. They're watching us all. Their knowing means we have to go. Soon."

"They'll force us to take the Tonic. They'll bend us back to what we were," Gideon said. "They'll use us up."

"So now we plan," Abigail said. "Then we leave."

"When?" I asked.

"Two nights from now," Gideon said. "After lights out, after everyone is asleep."

"We just have to get to the right people." Daniel turned to the computer. "Shiloh's owners. And maybe get help from Ms. Iverson."

A map came up on the screen.

"This is the city proper."

The photograph seemed to be a shot from the air, with buildings tiny as game pieces.

"Here's where we are."

A blinking triangle moved over a small black dot.

"That's Haven Hospital and Halls?" I asked.

He nodded.

"We have to get here. To the city building." He moved the arrow to the other side of the computer screen.

"How far is that?" Abigail asked. Her face looked ghostly. She gave me a halfhearted smile—one that didn't seem so unusual anymore—and I could see how nervous she was.

Was she thinking about the stone wall, the fence we had peered over? Was she wondering how we would all get over that? How would she? And what about Daniel? And then after that, how would I walk for miles? None of us was whole enough to do this except Gideon.

"Not too far," Gideon said. "A couple of miles. That's what it says here."

"How do we find help?"

Daniel didn't look away from the screen. "We go to Ann."

"There used to be a way to communicate over Interstar. We found the remains of it." Daniel made quotation marks in the air with his fingers when he said *remains*. "But that's all been disabled."

"Recently?" Abigail asked.

"We're not sure," Daniel said, shrugging.

"Look over the map, Shiloh," Gideon said. "Do you think you could memorize how to get to where we need to go?"

"It's not far, like you said. And the path is easy. But Haven Hospital and Halls is in a remote area. We're isolated out here."

"I'm exhausted," Abigail said. She was still worried. Her eyebrows worked together. I touched her hand, and her skin was clammy and cool.

"We can do this. We'll succeed," I said, but the words seemed a lie. I wasn't sure I believed them myself. "We have to hope. You said that yourself, Abigail."

Abigail said, "We all have to promise something." She put her arm around me, grabbed Daniel's hand.

"Sure," Daniel said. He held on to Abigail.

"We keep going, no matter what. We run for help, no matter what. No matter who is left behind, the others keep going."

"For the Terminals," Gideon said. He logged off the computer. The room grew dark.

"Just a minute, okay?" Daniel said. He spoke low, quiet. Not a thing like the Daniel I knew away from class. "We can do this. We've all done worse than running away. But if it comes to it . . ." Daniel moved in his wheelchair. "You leave me behind."

"We've already talked about this," Gideon said.

"I'm a burden, Gideon. I'll slow everyone down. You know it."

"I don't care what you say," Gideon said. "I'm not losing anyone else."

Something awful passed through me. I had worried about this very thing, and now here we were talking about it. What Daniel said made sense and that made my face burn from guilt.

"Me, too," Abigail said. "If I slow you down, you have to leave me behind, too. Whoever can, keeps going."

"No," I said. It felt as though someone strangled me.

"We all leave together." Sound went swirling down the hall and I waited to see if we would be found out. "We're letting people know we're *all* worthy to live. That *all* Terminals deserve a chance. *We* are doing it. Now I'm done with this tonight." Gideon left the room, disappearing so I couldn't see even a trace of him.

Abigail whispered, "We've been away too long. Dr. King may visit our room again."

"Shiloh." Daniel grabbed my wrist so tight, his grip hurt. "Think of the Cause. Gideon can't see past the personal. You're whole enough to make it. Don't let Gideon surrender just because he has a heart."

I thought of the Heart and Soul plants leaning in the morning breeze.

"I'm not sure any of us could leave someone behind," I said, shaking Daniel off me.

"We're going together, Daniel," Abigail said. She knelt in front of his wheelchair. "It's *all* of us or none of us." Her voice softened.

Daniel pulled Abigail up and she sat on his lap. Her arms went around his neck.

"We have to do what's good for *all* of us," he said. "If one of us doesn't make it, that's no big deal. If none of us make it, we fail."

"I can't leave you," Abigail said. "Gideon can't either, Daniel. We won't."

Daniel ran his fingers through Abigail's hair. She leaned her face close to his and he pressed his lips on Abigail's face. This wasn't like Ms. Iverson and Mr. Tremmel, but gentle and sad. I felt like we were stuck in a bottle. Strangled, like we didn't have a chance.

"Do what's best for the Cause," he said.

Abigail kissed Daniel again, then once more. When she stood, she kept a tight grip on his hand.

"Be able to let me go," he said. "For everyone."

Daniel rolled away, the whisper of the wheelchair all that I heard. He didn't get far when he stopped and swung around. "Be aware," he said. "For some reason, they've picked up on you."

Then he was gone.

I can't be asleep long, when I start awake.

What was it I heard? Outside the window, the sky is still dark, with no promise of morning. I'm tired and can't quite get my eyes open all the way.

Covers to my chin. Fingers curled around the cloth. Flat on my back.

Is it Abigail? Awake?

Then I see him there at the end of the bed. A male. Huge.

No face.

I try closing my eyes but there's no doing what I want.

He wants me to see him. Wants to frighten me.

Somehow, he's to the side of my bed without taking a step.

"Shiloh," he says. His voice is like water. "Shiloh."

Fingers touch my throat, and his skin on mine burns.

"You know better than to break the rules."

If I could move, I would nod. But his fire touch keeps me still. I want to call for Abigail. If I do, she's caught, too.

He bends so close I can see through the blackness.

Gideon.

"We won't leave anyone," he says. His lips are the color of a storm cloud. Gray as fireplace ash.

When he presses his mouth on mine, I think I might choke on the dust that surges past my teeth.

I thrash about, trying to push Gideon away.

But he's strong.

So strong. His hands are on my shoulders, burning me every place he caresses.

He climbs on top of me, the blanket between us, his teeth are on my throat.

And

I know I'm going to die.

22

Seeing Gideon at breakfast (though I pretended not to look) made my pulse quicken. Would he kill me like my dream said? I didn't even believe there was truth to dreams, so why did I care?

That was what the old Shiloh would think, the Shiloh drugged by the Tonic. It wasn't at all what the almost-free female Terminal would wonder. We were a team.

"Meet me," Gideon said when I left my breakfast dishes on the kitchen counter. Miss Maria stood near the conveyor belt, checking our food consumption. "Same time."

Miss Maria is large. Thick. "Good girl, Shiloh," she said. "Keep on working."

Her words slowed me midstep.

What did she mean by that? *Good girl*. What was that?

"Okay," I said, and moved off from the growing stack of used plates that slid into the kitchen.

Ahead, Gideon stuck his hands in his pockets and wandered away, not even waiting for an answer.

Terminals don't watch each other.

But, I noticed.

I noticed that Gideon stood straight and tall, looked at people, moved like the Whole did. I saw he made eye contact with Miss Maria.

Stop this. Get going. I need to get to class.

That image of him walking as though he wasn't a Terminal spread all through my body. Gideon wasn't like the rest of the Terminals. When I put my mind to it, I realized that I couldn't remember him ever having been out for Illness. Yes, he had spent time in Isolation. Plenty. But he'd never had an operation. Why not?

I tripped on nothing. There was too much the Tonic would have wiped out. Comments and attitudes. Nightmares and plans.

I had to keep going, head down, shuffling along. Be the same. I couldn't attract any more attention than I already had. There was too much at risk now.

Could Gideon be trusted?

I wanted to trust. I thought of him with the sun at his back. The warmth of his body. How tall he was. I shouldn't think anything negative against Gideon. I wouldn't. That was reckless and might cause me to falter. And faltering would never do.

"I have a new novel for you," Ms. Iverson said when math and Terminal history were over. "This is the story of the ultimate Terminal." She held a book aloft. "It's called *Invisible Man*."

The cover showed someone in bandages wearing dark glasses, his face concealed.

Camille said, "He's had something on his face removed."

"Close, Camille," Ms. Iverson said. "Let's see." She opened the book, pressed the cover back and read. "I am an invisible Terminal."

My pulse quickened.

We were invisible here. If we made it out, would the Whole see us? Would they take notice?

"This next line," Ms. Iverson said, "reminds me of Gideon."

A few of our classmates looked toward Gideon, who raised his head, propped his chin against his hand.

Ms. Iverson read on. "'I am a man of substance, of flesh and bone, fiber and liquids—and I might even be said to possess a mind—though not a soul. I am invisible, understand, simply because the Whole refuse to see me.'"

"They *don't* see us," he said. "Not really."

"Some might," I said, speaking out of turn.

177

"Not enough to step up for us and find the Cures we need." This was quiet Peter, who never says anything.

Ms. Iverson didn't answer. She started reading again.

The words were in my head. Sealed in cement. The only way I'd lose them was if I gave up.

I might even be said to possess a mind—though not a soul.

We had minds.

What about souls?

Good girl.

Miss Maria meant *me*. I wasn't sure about the girl part, but I knew what it meant to be good.

Because we were. We behaved. We tried. Did being good mean that we had worth? Not financial worth, but value enough to live a full life?

There was no one in here who had ever done a bad thing.

We were invisible, yes, because the Whole refused to see us.

"Some of the Whole," I said, speaking the words aloud, interrupting Ms. Iverson's reading.

Gideon looked back at me. So did Daniel.

"What do you mean, Shiloh?" Ms. Iverson asked, setting the book in her lap.

Not *one* person in this room had done anything wrong. "*You* see us, Ms. Iverson," I said.

She was quiet. And then she said, "Yes, I do, Shiloh."

"The temperature is dropping a bit," Gideon said. "This spring has been colder, longer, than normal." His voice came from a dark corner. I swung around to meet him.

"Want to go outside?"

"For what?"

"No reason, really. Maybe walk to the gazebo? You lead the way, so we can make sure you can do it."

I shrugged. "I can do it."

Gideon came up next to me and we headed down the hall. "You made a mistake today, calling her out like that."

Unease ran over my skin. "I know."

"Daniel isn't sure you're a part of us because of what you said."

"Of course I'm with you."

"Are you sure?" Gideon's voice was tentative. Did he feel the same way Daniel did? Did Abigail?

"The words came out. I tried to hold them in."

Nothing from Gideon.

"I swear it, Gideon. I want to help us all. And I didn't mean to draw attention. She seems someone we could trust."

"What if she's here as a plant?"

"She's part of the Planting Committee."

"No, Shiloh. Plants get information."

"I don't understand."

"A plant is anyone put in a situation to learn information. Maybe Ms. Iverson's nice because Dr. King wants her to find stuff out about *us*."

"How do you know that?"

Gideon thought. "Good question. I just seem to know it. Maybe Adam told me."

"You mean your Adam. *Your* Recipient."

He dropped his head a little.

"Dr. King couldn't save him," I said. "Something happened. Like with my Recipient. Adam was too far gone and Dr. King couldn't save him."

The thought knocked at my brain. Dr. King's own words. *Couldn't* save him. And then there were Abigail's words that Dr. King didn't succeed 100 percent of the time.

"Let's go," Gideon said. "Let's see if you know the way."

We headed south, through the fire door to the stairwell. Down stairs. Farther south. A right. Another right and then a left. And there we were, to a basement door that led outside. We were at the end of the building closest to the gazebo.

"Good," Gideon said, and he let out a sigh. "You're doing great, Shiloh."

Good girl.

"If something happens to me or Daniel, remember how to get out of here then go for help."

"Nothing will happen."

"I know," Gideon said. "But if you needed to get Abigail out of here without me or Daniel, you could do it."

"We're going together. All four of us." I stomped to the gazebo. I could see the astilbe bending, nodding their budding heads, their leaves waving. There was a first quarter moon high in the sky. It was white, bright. "Maybe we shouldn't be out here."

"I wanted to be with you, Shiloh." Gideon took my hand and led me to the chairs under the latticed ceiling. Once, I sat out here with Abigail. We were both little. So little that our feet didn't touch the ground when we sat. Strange that Haven Hospital & Halls would have something that made us ill. No older Terminal could sit here with someone else.

Gideon's arms went around me and he tugged me up to his chest.

"What are you doing?" I asked, but I didn't move away. Instead, I stood there stiff and let his arms encircle me.

His face bent closer to mine. Closer. And

a wave of shock shot through me when Gideon's lips touched right above my own.

He was kissing me? I should fight! Run from this way of spreading germs! I'd dreamed this—perhaps now my dream was coming true and my life would be sucked from my body!

But this was not like getting your life sucked from you. My legs turned to oil and I had a hard time standing. I *needed* to lean into Gideon. His lips touched mine again. *This* was why Ms. Iverson let Mr. Tremmel kiss her and why Abigail kissed Daniel.

"I'm glad we're here together." His arms tightened around me and I stood there unsure of what to do. A light rain fell like it didn't mean it. Gideon's words were on my forehead, warming my skin. "You can put your arms around me, if you want."

"Should I?" I moved my arms around his waist. Let my face rest against his jacket. The rain fell through the lattice above us.

My raw nerves settled. I felt . . . what? Safe?

The next kiss lasted longer, this time right on my mouth, lips parted so I felt Gideon's breath on my teeth.

Terminals needed to touch. We needed to know comfort. Maybe touch could save us.

Or make us rebel.

I relaxed more into Gideon. My mind loosened, too. "Gideon, why do you seem Whole?"

He pulled back. "What do you mean?"

"You're different. Without the Tonic, I see that. And you weren't reported for throwing the chair. You had Adam when the rest of us had our Keepers taken away. Why?"

Gideon didn't say anything for a long time. "I'm not sure, Shiloh." The words came out in a steamy cloud. Then he kissed me again.

HAVEN
HOSPITAL&HALLS
Where You Matter
Established 2020

Note to all Staff

Any and all staff found assisting Terminals in rebellion will be terminated.

23

That night, when I was back in the room with one last kiss, I lay in bed thinking.

Of all the Terminals, there were two who seemed to have no risk. Me, because my Recipient mother wouldn't allow it. And Gideon because of Adam.

And Dr. King allowed *that*.

Or maybe, I thought, as sleep overtook me, we were the most at risk because of those things.

"Shiloh?"

I felt a bit of a smile (a smile—on me?) when I saw Gideon.

He walked toward me, fast, Terminal females staring at him, moving to get out of his way.

"You shouldn't be in the Females' Hallway area," someone said.

"Why are you here, Gideon?" Abigail sounded surprised.

"No questions," he said to her. "I got caught." He turned and walked away, toward the Dining Hall where we were all headed.

"Wait." I started after Gideon, but Abigail grabbed my arm.

"No," she said. "We know nothing."

The last of the females heading to breakfast split apart around us, shuffling along, tense expressions on their faces.

"I knew this would happen," Abigail said. "I knew it. Act normal. Act Terminal."

I could smell breakfast omelets. The sweet odor of cooked onions. My stomach growled.

Abigail didn't move her lips when she spoke. "What do you think happened?" There was panic in Abigail's voice and her alarm scared me.

"I don't know." The floor felt uneven under my feet.

Terminals, male and female, met in the foyer outside the Dining Hall and were going through the double doors to their proper sides of the room. I didn't search for where the Teachers were. Where Dr. King was.

Morning light splashed through the window. Bright. White. Cool looking.

Some Terminals lined up for their meals.

Dr. King came into the Dining Hall. His eyes caught mine and I dropped my gaze.

But I had seen it. Had seen the same look of confidence he wore in commercials on his face now. My mouth dried out.

I licked my lips. They felt hot from last night's kiss. No. That couldn't be.

Hands shaking, I got my breakfast, and keeping my steps as slow as I could, went to the table. There was little sound in the room. Just forks against plates, glasses being set on the table.

"It's not lunch," Matthew said. His voice came across the tables to where I usually sit with Abigail and Ruth. Ms. Iverson jerked her head up and she touched her throat.

The doors. The doors were opening during breakfast.

"It's not lunch. It's not." The murmur went around the room. Even Teachers were surprised.

I sat, almost dropping my tray.

"What are they doing here now?" I heard Ms. Iverson ask. "It's not been that long since the last removal. Why are they here now?"

Mr. MacGee hushed her. His hand went to his chest, like he was checking his own pulse.

Abigail poked at the omelet on her plate.

This was bad. Maybe the female, Ann, had lost the battle. Across the room, Gideon looked at me. Dr. King walked over and said something to him and Gideon nodded.

My heart slowed as the doors opened like a mouth, and Principal Harrison came through them alone, carrying the manila envelope.

"Hello, Terminals," Dr. King said, walking over to join Principal Harrison. He adjusted his glasses, but his face was without emotion. He took the paperwork. "This is a different way to start the day, isn't it?"

Principal Harrison rocked on his heels as he always did.

Start counting, my mind commanded but this time I wouldn't.

I pressed my palms hard into my cheekbones so I wouldn't have to see anything—even if I was the one they took.

"Shiloh!" Abigail's whispered voice reached for me, but I shook my head at her. I couldn't look. I shouldn't look. Fear filled me. Rushed through my veins like a river might. Something was desperately wrong.

"There has been a change of plans," Dr. King said into the microphone. I heard the envelope as it flapped in the air from him waving it around.

I grabbed Abigail's hand, not caring who saw.

"Don't do that," Ruth said. "Abigail, Shiloh. No. Touching makes me sick."

"We may have a bit of an epidemic." Dr. King spoke on. "I know this is unusual. Someone last week and now this week and at breakfast, too."

Abigail squeezed my hand. And I knew. I shook myself free of her. Pushed back my chair. Hands trembling against the table.

"Daniel." The name echoed in my head. Several Terminals stared at me. Ms. Iverson waved me to sit down. Her face was blotchy.

"Daniel," Dr. King said. "Oh, and Abigail."

The air went soft as cotton. That cotton got caught in my throat. In my lung. In my eyes and under my nails. I couldn't move.

"Shiloh, sit down." My knees refused to bend. "Daniel, Abigail, after your meals, please come to the front office. Someone will be waiting. You'll each need your prepared bag. I said sit down, Shiloh."

There was no sound in the room. All the Terminals, all the Teachers, everyone was silent.

"No!"

The scream caught me off guard. I clutched my throat.

Was it me? Was I the one screaming?

Principal Harrison strode toward Gideon, who leapt to his feet and sprinted to Daniel.

"Run, Abigail!" I screamed so it felt like my throat ripped. "Run!"

Abigail jumped to her feet. Gideon ran for Daniel. Principal Harrison moved like a cat. He slipped, fell to one knee. "Go. Go! Daniel, go!" Abigail's voice was shrill. I saw a Terminal cover her ears.

Daniel backed his chair away from the table, spun out on the shiny floor, caught traction, and peeled away. Gideon ran behind him, grabbed the wheelchair handles, and pushed Daniel toward the doors.

The Dining Hall erupted. Teachers stood, looked around as though they weren't sure where to go. Terminals hid under the tables, some ran, a few fought Teachers. Dishes crashed to the floor. Everything came to life around us—more life than any of these Terminals had ever seen.

"Go," I said to Abigail, giving her a push. "Go, go go!" And she did. She stepped onto her chair and ran down the length of the table, her arm held out for balance. Two Terminals followed, climbing on the tabletops. One female fell. Then several Terminals screamed. The younger males and females called out for help, mouths open wide in tearless crying.

Terminals blocked those Teachers who ran at Abigail and Gideon and Daniel. Mr. MacGee and Dr. King both grabbed at Gideon, who managed to twist away.

Abigail made it to the Dining Hall doors, which crashed shut almost in her face.

"Iverson, get your ward," Principal Harrison hollered. But Ms. Iverson looked down at her plate as though none of this were happening around her.

He caught Abigail in the corner, grabbed and jerked her around. He pulled her arm up behind her back. The lunchroom was pandemonium. Someone bellowed for quiet. Ms. Iverson jumped up, ran to Principal Harrison.

Abigail got free, swung at him, hitting him under the eye.

I ran then, screaming as I went. "Abigail!" Principal Harrison pushed her to the floor. He swung back, knocking Ms. Iverson off her feet.

Mr. Tremmel appeared out of nowhere. He pulled Ms. Iverson to safety.

"Help Abigail!" She was screaming. "Paul, help Abigail!"

But Mr. Tremmel locked his arms about Ms. Iverson and pulled her close.

The doors burst open and Security swarmed in the room. Two males, huge males, trapped Abigail.

Terminals rushed around.

"It's okay," Principal Harrison said like he was crooning a song. "It's okay, Abigail. You are all right. Safe." He pulled her to a standing position.

"Let her go," I said. "Fight, Abigail. Fight."

Someone knocked me to the ground and I saw it was Dr. King. I couldn't get up. The air was gone. I couldn't even sit.

"Shiloh," Abigail said. Tears streamed down her face. Dr. King scooped her into his arms but she hit and kicked. "Shiloh!"

My eyes and nose burned. I coughed.

Abigail was leaving. Both Gideon and Daniel had been stopped, too. They were on the floor, facedown. Arms locked behind them. The room was a mess. Teachers tried to calm Terminals. Only a few tried to help Gideon and me and Abigail and Daniel. Several threw up.

Let her stay, please, I wanted to say. A bit of air crept in my chest. I gasped, trying to relax.

Behind me, I heard Gideon call out my name.

My fingers tingled and my lips felt numb.

"Get him out of here!" Principal Harrison hollered at Mr. Mac-Gee. "To your room, Shiloh."

But I ignored everyone.

"Don't let them take me, Shiloh."

"Don't give up," I said.

Principal Harrison said, "You're going to be okay, Abigail." He looked at me. "Make this easier, Shiloh. Let her leave the room with dignity."

Teachers cornered the aggressive Terminals. Others hushed the rest of my schoolmates. Security dragged Gideon from the room. I could hear him yelling to keep fighting all the way down the hall. Where was Daniel now?

Abigail hit the principal until he gave her a sharp shake. Then he carried her from the Dining Hall. When I tried to crawl toward her, Dr. King grabbed me and jerked me backwards so hard, I felt my neck snap.

"That's not necessary, sir." Ms. Iverson touched my arm. It felt cool in the heat on my skin.

Abigail was gone.

I slumped to the floor. A few young Terminals wailed. Someone called for backup.

But that wasn't necessary.

The Terminals had been defeated.

24

I was in Isolation. I could smell it. The room was white, and cold, and I was on the floor. There was nothing in here, not even a seam to show me where the door was. No lock. No window. No bed or pillow or blanket.

I sat up, scooted till I leaned against the wall, and rested against the coolness of the plaster. My eyes were hot inside the sockets. My brain felt like it burned. My skin, all of it, was so sensitive, I couldn't touch it. My clothes felt like sandpaper.

What had happened? Why was I here? Little by little I remembered.

Dr. King. Principal Harrison.

"No." My mouth, lips, tongue, even my teeth felt swollen.

Abigail was gone. Daniel, too.

That fight. That huge fight. That we lost.

I couldn't swallow. What about Gideon, where was he? Had he gotten free? Had anyone?

The side of my head ached, and when I touched it, I felt a lump.

I remembered Dr. King's fingers squeezing into my shoulders when he came into my room later. The way he had said, "I don't care who may have paid for you to be cloned, Shiloh, you will die."

I refused to think of it.

I wouldn't give up.

I would keep fighting, like Gideon said.

When I stood, my neck felt like string. Pain pounded all through me. Where was the corner? Putting my hands out, I touched the wall. It was smooth as glass. It would be hard to know where I'd started, so I took my shirt off and dropped it on the floor. Then began the slow process of going around the room, so sick, I felt it would have been better never to fight.

"You've been to Isolation before." My voice echoed. I put my shirt back on and sat down. I would wait.

I'm not sure how much time passed. Security brought me Tonic. That was different. Why Security? Several times I faked drinking the stuff, taking off my jeans and spitting the liquid into the back pocket where it dried to a crust.

I slept on the floor, cold. Everything burned like my incision had, my stomach tumbled over itself, my fingernails broke against the floor, the walls, looking for the entrance I knew was here somewhere.

Male and female Security came in the Isolation room together again and again, forcing me to drink the Tonic. How did they know?

I spit out as much as I could. But they were stronger. The Whole are always stronger.

Now the headache bloomed bright as fireworks. It spread everywhere. I felt it in my toenails, my eyelashes, the skin on my calves. Why so intense?

If I got out of here, I would fight back.

No, *when* I got out of here, I would fight back.

I would.

I held my hands over my ears to stop the pain.

If the ache went away, I would fight back.

I would.

For Abigail. For Daniel and Gideon. For every Terminal.

For me.

I would fight back.

I would.

Maybe.

The hall is as white and cold as snow. It's slippery as ice. I can't stand up. So I crawl.

In one corner there is Tonic, like blood. I run my finger through it to mark my place. Crawl until I'm in the operation room. It takes hours. Years.

Dr. King, big as life, holds a spade. Gideon is on the operating table. He looks at me.

"Shiloh," he says, "help."

Dr. King raises the spade.

"Shiloh."

There is dirt on the edge of the blade.

"Get free."

Dr. King swings the tool down with all his might.

There's a thump. A splatter.

The sounds makes my head crash in on itself.

Gideon says nothing.

Blood leaks from his mouth, a drop at a time.

I mark my spot in the deep red liquid.

25

"Shiloh."

My head pounded.

"Shiloh."

I looked around the room. I'd gone blind. When I peered at my own hands, I seemed washed out. Pale. Was I fading away?

Words pressed close.

"I'm going to get you out. I'll get you free."

"Gideon?"

"I'm outside the door. Be quiet. I wanted to make sure where you were."

I heard the turning of a key and there appeared in the wall a rectangle of darkness the color of ink.

"Come toward my voice, Shiloh. Hurry."

"I can't see," I said. I felt hot, too hot to move, like only bones and skin were left of me.

"It's just the lights," Gideon said. "Recovery won't be so bad this time."

When he reached for my hand my head swirled. I heaved.

"You've only been in here a few days, the Tonic won't be so hard to come off. We've got to go."

"I can't."

My legs are done moving. I crawled too far.

Gideon was close. His touch burned the meat from the bones of my face. "You have to go. *We* have to go. They got everyone but me."

I tried to stand and staggered.

You don't have to go with him, my head said. But I did. I remembered that. I had to go because Gideon was fighting for the Terminals. And so was Abigail, my best friend.

"*I'm* fighting for the Terminals," I said.

Gideon slipped his arm around my waist, then he hugged me. I lifted my arms, heavy as trees, and put them around his neck.

This was what I had wanted to do all along. Even when I was full of Tonic and didn't know I wanted it, this was what I wanted. Someone to hold me.

My eyes stung with tears.

Gideon helped me walk, closed the door with a click, and the world fell into a deep quiet.

"I'm surprised there's no guard," he said. "I guess he didn't think I'd try to get you." He handed me something to drink. "Here."

"No."

"This will help. I knew it was here. Adam told me. I found it when I came to get you. Drink the whole thing."

"Too much. I can't." Focusing was hard. The bottle seemed huge. Far too much for one Terminal to drink.

Gideon put his hands on either side of my face. "It will cure you, Shiloh."

My eyes buzzed. "Promise?"

He nodded and uncapped the drink. "They give this to us to help us get ready for the operations. It clears the Tonic out of the blood. You'll be better in an hour. And if you can walk now . . ."

I drank the liquid down as fast as I could. It smelled like plants, was the color of dirt, and tasted bitter. But it soothed me, made the pain not-so-quite-there. I swallowed it all, then gave the container back to Gideon.

Where were we? Isolation was in the Infirmary building. But I couldn't remember getting here. "Where is he?"

"Dr. King? I don't know. Maybe looking for me. Maybe not. He doesn't think I'll do anything to stop him. We've had a little talk."

"You spoke to him? What about?"

"He asked why we fought. Wondered what our connections are."

"What did you say?"

"I pretended like I didn't know a thing. But he knows I do." Gideon pulled me closer in a sideways hug. "Don't worry, Shiloh. I'm not good enough for him. I have no soul."

"Neither does Dr. King," I said.

Gideon put his lips on mine and I didn't fight him. I let him press against me, feeling my body warm. His mouth was hot on mine. I reached for his face, ran my palms over his skin. So warm. And smooth, too. He pulled away and I touched his throat, touched the line of his jaw. I put my hand on the back of his neck.

"Do that again," I said. And he did, pulling me so close, I felt his heart beating.

Were your heart and soul the same thing? If you had a heart, did you have a soul?

Gideon let me loose and, holding tight to each other, we started down the hall.

Even after the long walk from Isolation, with him supporting me as we went, I remembered Gideon's lips on mine. My brain fought to clear itself. I felt the drink coursing through my body. The aches in my skin left first, in my joints next, and finally, finally the burning pain in my face and head was gone. There was that same residual feeling I'd felt the first time off the Tonic, the jarring flashes of light when I moved fast, but I was careful and took light steps.

And still I thought of kissing Gideon.

We went downstairs. Would he kiss me again? I stood on tiptoe, wanting him to, and he leaned his face toward mine. He ran his fingers over my cheekbone.

"We have to see if we can rescue the others. He has them." He folded me in his arms. I heard him swallow.

If it all ends for me, I thought, my face pressed into Gideon's jacket, *it was worth this little bit of being normal.*

The hall was empty. At the end a door stood wide open.

"That's his office."

"Dr. King's here?"

"Must be."

I did not want to do this. "What time is it?"

Gideon shrugged. "It took me awhile to find you."

"And the others?" In my mind I saw Abigail's face, saw her begging me to keep her safe, to not let them take her. "Gideon? Why are you here?" The question came out a whisper.

"Adam. I guess Adam." He shook his head. "I don't know."

The recovery room was so clean, I couldn't smell anything.

They have no souls.

It isn't human.

She looks like Victoria.

Someone lay on the bed. Part of someone. I pressed my hands to my eyes. Tried to block what I saw.

"Abigail?" I stumbled forward. Yes. There she was and wasn't. Oh. No no no. "Abigail."

Why had this happened? My eyes couldn't make sense of things.

Go to her.

My feet propelled me until I stood near Abigail's bed.

I wanted to say her name again, but my mouth didn't open.

She was suspended a few inches above the mattress, held together by wires and cords and plugs. She seemed to float. Like those eyes in the jar.

I made myself speak. "I'm with you." Could she hear me? Her face was slack, her lips formed a grimace like something caused her pain. What was left of her hair was caught up in a net. The braid was gone. "Gideon and me. We're . . ." We're what? "We're getting help. We're getting out of here and we're getting help. We're going for the female in the video, for Ann. We'll find her and I'll come back for you." I spoke fast.

A plastic tube ran from Abigail's side onto a cloth on the coverlet.

Just a gentle tug here, Shiloh.

Ouch, that hurts, that hurts.

I know it does.

A cool hand on my forehead.

The drain's gone now and soon you'll be good as new.

I touched the scar on my side near where my lung had been.

That's when I cried. So hard, I had to cover my mouth to keep the sound tight to me. I leaned against the bed where Abigail lay. The stand, holding the bag of fluids that ran into her one arm, rattled.

"It isn't fair," I said. I covered my face, lay my head on the sheet near her, and wept. "It isn't."

Whoever said a Terminal's life is fair? came into my mind. No one! No one said anything for a Terminal!

Gideon and Daniel were right. We had to save ourselves.

I stroked Abigail's cheek, leaving a damp line of my tears.

"Shiloh." Gideon's voice sounded like it perched on my shoulder. "I'm going to see if I can find Daniel. I'll be back. Stay quiet. Dr. King is close."

The whole time Gideon was gone, I stood near Abigail and cried. I touched her skin, cool under my fingers.

"It will be okay," I said. Where had that lie come from? It wouldn't be okay. Things would never be the same again. Because here was Abigail, right here, and she couldn't move and she wouldn't be able to get away with us and she wasn't even complete anymore. She was just pieces. That's all. A monitor showed the rhythm of her forced breathing, another the beating of her heart.

Her heart.

Her heart and soul.

Panic started in my chest, fluttering like butterflies, then turned to a swarm of bees.

"I swear it will be okay, Abigail. We'll get help."

"This isn't good, Shiloh," Gideon said. "Abigail doesn't look good at all." His voice cracked and his eyes were red. "We have to go. We need to move before someone finds out we're gone. There's no time."

"Did you find Daniel?"

Gideon shook his head.

I said, "I can't leave her." The bees had flown to my voice box and hid the sound with their buzzing. "She'll be alone."

"No," he said, his voice low and soothing. "No, she'll be safe here. Someone will check on her. I promise. They're keeping her alive."

He looked at me and I could see the lies in what he said, could see that he recognized those lies, too.

"She'll never get away now." I turned to him, my head swimming with the movement. "We've got to take her with us when we go. Tell me we can."

He clasped my shoulders. "She'll die for sure if we take her. And so will we. We can't be burdened with someone we have to carry."

"But . . ."

Gideon looked away. I knew what he was thinking.

Daniel.

Someone we had to carry.

How would we move Daniel if we found him? If he was this bad? If he was worse?

Abigail's mouth was strained, lips pulled back in pain, teeth clenched. What had they done to make her face like that?

Had she fought the way she did in the Dining Hall?

"We have to go."

"Okay," I said, and I leaned over and pressed my lips to her face. She was cool cool cool, her skin soft. "We'll come back for her? Right? Promise me."

He didn't even pause. "Yes, Shiloh. We will." And this time there was no lie in his voice.

26

"What are you two doing?"

I squeezed my eyes shut, pulling the door closed to Abigail's room behind me. My hands tightened to fists.

Dr. King stood there in the hallway. He looked huge. "Gideon," he said. "Shiloh. What a surprise. You both know these buildings are off-limits." Dr. King sounded distressed. Not angry at all. And he looked so disappointed. It felt like all the good air was sucked away when Dr. King walked into the room. I tried not to be afraid, but I was.

Gideon's face didn't change. I should touch him. Pull some of his calmness into myself. Could either one of them see my pulse pounding in my throat?

Gideon didn't respond to my touch. He just straightened. Stood taller. Like he had waited for this moment when we would stand face-to-face with Dr. King.

"We're looking for Daniel, Dr. King," Gideon said. His voice was matter-of-fact. Like this was part of his duties as a Terminal. "We can't leave him behind."

"You're such a good Terminal, Gideon, thinking of your fellow beings." He gave a sad smile. "Just like Adam. He was so much like you." Dr. King shook his head, as though he couldn't believe how similar Adam and Gideon were.

"Don't talk about him," Gideon said. "He *was* good."

"Adam," Dr. King said, "was amazing. The best thing I ever did."

Gideon said, "You had nothing to do with him. Adam was himself. He was one of the Whole who stood up for us all."

"Stood up for the Terminals?" Dr. King nodded. "Yes. And that was his undoing. He couldn't be saved, nor could his mother. Even with all this technology, he couldn't be saved." Dr. King gestured to the hall we stood in.

"You don't save Terminals," I said. "You use them to death."

"You're right, Shiloh. But Adam was not just some Whole male. He was my flesh and blood. He was my son."

What?

Gideon said, "I don't understand."

"It's just what I said, Gideon. Adam was my child. He should have been your Recipient. But he became the only Whole I couldn't save because he wouldn't *let* me. Nor would his mother. They were against the work I did."

Gideon's hand found mine. His fingers were cold. "That can't be true."

"But it is." Dr. King seemed to slump in on himself. He shrunk before my eyes. "He grew attached to you. And when he was old enough, he signed a waiver preventing me from using you to make him better in any way."

"And then there was the accident," I said.

Dr. King straightened. "This is hardly your business," he said. He turned to Gideon. "I'll let you off with this offense, Gideon," he said, "because that's what Adam would have wanted. But Shiloh—" He smiled, showing only his bottom teeth. "—you belong in the Isolation room. The mother of your Recipient would be appalled to know of this misdemeanor."

"We're leaving," I said.

"I keep you all in the finest of circumstances." Dr. King waved his hand around like this gesture would show all he had done for the Terminals. "Why would you even consider such a thing? Do you know how lucky you are to be in *this* hospital? In other hospitals, the Replicants are kept in cages. Kept like chickens, crammed together, uneducated. Treatment here is ethical. It's good."

"We're a product," I said.

Gideon stood silent, like his words had been stolen from him.

Dr. King pursed his lips. "Not all of you. Your Daniel, for example. *He* wants to stay here."

"That's not true," Gideon said.

"You may speak to him yourself. I was checking on him when the two of you—" Dr. King waved his hands around. "—entered the building illegally."

"Where is he?" Gideon's voice was strained.

"Go have a word with Daniel. Then you'll see how you can benefit others if you so choose."

Dr. King led us to a room at the end of the hall. We all stood in
the doorway.

"As you can see," Dr. King said, "he has legs."

Gideon didn't move. It was like he was stuck. I stepped forward,
to where Daniel lay on the bed. Unlike Abigail, he looked—what?
Alive? Yes, that was it.

"He made a trade. Legs for valuable information."

"What do you mean?" Gideon asked.

Daniel appeared to be asleep. The odor of sickness filled the room.

"You know." Again Dr. King waved his hand and when he did, I
saw Gideon in the movement. "*I* gave him a pair of legs. He let me
know your plans. We've been communicating for some time."

"That's not true," Gideon said, the words one-at-a-time slow.

"Oh, it is," Dr. King said. "It is." He sounded jovial. "We just
need to see if this works. We've never done anything this big before.
It's a graft, of sorts. Not a match at all. Someone else's legs. You may
remember Isaac?"

Lightning flashed through me.

"Of course, I think we'll be successful."

"Daniel?" I whispered his name, and Daniel's eyes opened. The
smell got worse as I neared him.

"Shiloh," he said. I could hear how weak he was. "I don't feel
well. I need something to drink."

I held a plastic cup filled with ice and water to Daniel's lips. He
sipped the drink.

"Better?"

With his glasses off, Daniel's eyes looked bigger than normal,
glassy. He looked in the direction of Dr. King and Gideon. "Come
closer," he said.

"No company secrets, now," Dr. King said. "Go talk to your best friend, Gideon. Adam would want you to."

"No, thank you," Gideon said, and he turned away.

I bent over Daniel. I could feel the fever radiating from him. "I made a mistake," he said. "No matter what Dr. King tells you, I made a mistake. Let everyone know."

"I will," I said. "I promise."

"If I get out of this, Shiloh, I'll be there to help the Terminals. Tell Gideon I said so, will you?"

"Yes," I said. "Of course, Daniel." I touched his forehead with the back of my hand. "He's burning up."

Dr. King walked to the side of the bed. He checked a few readings on the equipment Daniel was hooked up to. "If the fever breaks," Dr. King said, "we have a new success. You win a few, you lose a few with Terminal experimentation. But it's all for the good of the Whole. We're always a step ahead here at Haven Hospital and Halls."

I felt sick to my stomach. "You promised him . . ."

Behind me, Gideon cleared his throat.

"Let's go, Shiloh," Dr. King said. He slapped his hands together. "We don't want to weary our patient."

"Remember me, okay, Shiloh?"

I nodded, squeezed Daniel's hand that felt fiery and dry in my own. "Always."

In the hall, with the door closed, I turned to Dr. King. Gideon stood away from us, his back toward me.

I caught my breath, bit it off. "I don't believe Daniel traded you anything. Not like you say."

Dr. King walked in slow motion toward the hall desk. He sat down and fingered an iris. It was a beautiful lavender. There had to be a dozen flowers in the vase. "You're very astute, Shiloh. A lot like Ann Alexander."

Starting, I spoke. "You fooled him. Like you've fooled the world into thinking we're something we aren't. You promised him something you couldn't deliver. You've killed Daniel and you killed Isaac, just to try to figure out what we were doing."

"I've not fooled anyone," Dr. King said. "I've given the Whole what they want. Eternal life. Eternal youth. Or as close as you can get. We live in a world where looking young reigns supreme."

"But you tricked Daniel."

"I offered him what he wanted," Dr. King said. "We've had rebellions before, you know. Adam started a few. We know what to keep an eye out for. I saw it coming with Daniel and knew what the trade should be." He folded his hands on the desktop. "The possibility of legs."

Gideon kept his back turned to us both. "You know what he would want."

Dr. King looked at Gideon. "I *gave* him what he wanted."

"Not Daniel," he said. "I'm not talking about Daniel."

Dr. King said nothing.

"We saw him. You keep his body still."

"You had no right—" Dr. King swelled up like a balloon.

"You care about him." Gideon took my hand and I could feel him trembling. "That's why you've let me live, and why you couldn't honor what he wanted—to be allowed to die. That's why he's hooked up to a bunch of monitors that live for him."

"Don't speak about my boy."

"I loved him, too," Gideon said. "Maybe not like you did, but I understood him and he—"

"You understood nothing of my son." The irises fell to the floor, the vase shattering. "You knew nothing of him."

Gideon walked closer to Dr. King, pulling me along. "I knew everything about him. I *am* him. You said so yourself. He and I talked all

205

the time. He told me how great you are. What a genius you are and how you could change the world. And he told me you believed in choice."

Dr. King was quiet. His mouth hung open.

"I believed Adam about you for a long time," Gideon said. "Now half of us are gone. And Shiloh and me, we're leaving."

Those last words hung in the air.

Gideon pulled me along, walking in a determined way, but I could still feel his hand shaking.

"You're worth too much," Dr. King said. "I can't let you go. I have business partners. I have bills. Accountability to others."

Gideon didn't slow. He hurried me along, tucked his arm into mine.

"Don't look back," Gideon said under his breath. "Whatever you do, just keep moving."

Down the corridor we went. A turn to the left. Dr. King's footsteps not following. His voice growing dim. "No matter what my son wanted, I'll not let you get away." Deeper into the basement.

"Go, go, go," I said.

A siren wailed. Then another. And another.

Gideon ran then, pulling me behind him. Out the door marked by the EXIT sign. Into the night. Up the stairs and across the lawn.

Sirens pealed and lights flashed.

Dr. King was there (how?), and Principal Harrison. Security spilled from the buildings, but we were ahead of them.

"Hurry, hurry."

Gideon dragged me. I didn't waste energy to speak. Just ran.

Miss Maria stepped from the shadows. "This way. This way."

"Follow her," I said to Gideon. We ran after Miss Maria, who took us to the front gate, where Ms. Iverson waited in a car for us to climb the fence to safety.

206

27

"Are you sure you can't go with us?" I asked Ms. Iverson. My nerves jangled. I was positive my very heart shook.

"Ann wants *you*," Ms. Iverson said. "Not me. Anyway, I need to get back to school so they don't suspect I had anything to do with your escape. I'm in trouble enough for fighting for you. We have to drop you here. It means you walking a bit, but we can't risk getting caught."

Miss Maria said, "They won't miss us if we're back in a few minutes. Go. The two of you. As soon as we can, we'll be back."

"It's almost morning," Ms. Iverson said. "I'll call her so she knows you're coming. Go to the address we gave you."

"1501 Cherry Lane," I said.

They both nodded.

We were a mile from Ann Alexander's home. I remembered from the map. But it seemed a forever from where Ms. Iverson had let us out. Every time a car slowed, I was sure Dr. King would leap out for us. I walked with my head down until Gideon said, "You look like a Terminal, Shiloh. Stand up straight and tall. That's the first thing I learned from Adam."

Be a Terminal. Look like a Terminal. Now look like the Whole. Maybe I would never fit in this world out here.

If they would even have us.

When I saw the house, I couldn't quite move.

We waited on the corner as the sky turned a golden yellow from the sun and then that heartbreaking blue. A warm breeze blew from the east and I tucked my hands into my jeans pockets.

"I think you should go alone," Gideon said.

His suggestion startled me.

"This is your moment. I had mine with Adam." Gideon took my hand and pressed his lips to my knuckles. Maybe I could stand here with Gideon the rest of my life, letting him touch me. Touching him. "You go."

I was silent.

Gideon's arms slipped around my waist and he hugged me, bending over a little so his face was close to mine.

"I'm ready," I said at last. The words were airless.

I crossed the street, looking once over my shoulder to Gideon, who lifted his hand.

"You'll have to knock, Shiloh," I reminded myself. And when I did, it seemed at first too soft, and then far too loud. Especially this early in the morning. From somewhere down the road, a dog barked.

It took forever before I heard the sound of footsteps. I knocked again. The door swung open enough for me to see only a part of her face, the male right behind her.

The woman in my dreams.

I've changed my mind.

"Shiloh?"

Don't change your mind.

"Shiloh?"

The door shut and I turned to Gideon.

She didn't want me.

I heard locks being released. The door opened.

"Oh, Shiloh," Ann said. "You look just like I thought you would. Just like my Victoria."

Ann's real voice—not something twisted from my memory, not a video, but her real voice. Her.

The sun crested the horizon, splashing light on us all.

I closed my eyes and remembered Abigail calling my name. I

could see her face, hear her talk about hope. About the Cause. I saw Daniel and Adam and Claudia and Elizabeth and Isaac. I saw Gideon.

"Shiloh," Ann said. "Come in."

She opened her arms to me.

HAVEN
HOSPITAL&HALLS
Where You Matter
Established 2020

Welcome to:

Daniel Smith—Faculty
Abigail Brown—Staff

HAVEN
HOSPITAL & HALLS
Where You Matter
Established 2020

Note to all Staff

Please make sure you are present for removals.